150
Things to Make and Do with Peppa

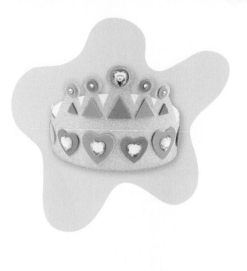

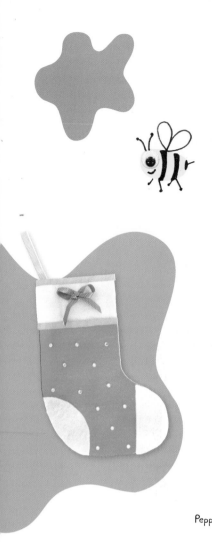

A GOLDEN BOOK · NEW YORK

eOne™   ASTLEY · BAKER · DAVIES

This book is based on the TV series Peppa Pig.
Peppa Pig is created by Neville Astley and Mark Baker.
Peppa Pig © Astley Baker Davies Ltd/Entertainment One UK Ltd 2003.
www.peppapig.com

ISBN 978-0-593-37406-1

rhcbooks.com

Printed in the United States of America

10 9 8 7 6 5 4 3 2

2020 Golden Books Edition

Peppa Pig™

150

Things to Make and Do with Peppa

How to Use this Book

The activities in this book have been created and written for big piggies to do with their little piggies and include plenty of ideas for games to play and for fun days out, as well as for things to make and bake.

All of the activities require some level of supervision, depending on the age and ability of your little piggy. For example, while older children will be able to manage some of the craft activities with minimal supervision, younger children will need close supervision at all times and many of the steps should be done for them. No matter what the age and ability of your child, **always** do yourself any steps that involve the use of an oven, scissors, or knives.

Although all the activities in this book require adult help, those that need particularly close supervision have been given the following icon:

Templates

Templates are included for some of the craft activities. Either photocopy the templates onto poster board or trace onto tracing paper (or parchment paper) and glue onto poster board before cutting them out.

Craft Activity Tips and Techniques

★ Let your little piggy help decide which activity to do, so you can talk about what you need and the best time (and place) to do it.

★ Make sure you have everything you need and enough time to complete each activity before you begin.

★ Start a collection of craft materials, such as scraps of fabric or tissue paper, old buttons, and recycled boxes, bottles, and toilet-paper rolls.

★ Invest in some strong, good-quality glue. As well as being good for sticking, it makes a good varnish when mixed with water–paint a coat on a finished, dry papier-mâché or salt-dough model so it looks shiny and lasts longer. (The glue will look milky at first but dries to a clear, hard finish.)

★ Protect any work surfaces, and make sure your little piggy is wearing an apron or an old T-shirt so they can have lots of messy fun.

★ Do any steps that require adult help, but try to let your child do as much of each activity as possible, such as painting or gluing. Try not to take over too much!

★ Don't forget to give plenty of praise and encouragement–including getting your little piggy to help clean up afterward!

Story Time

If you want a quiet, non-messy activity, try one of the story-starter activities to spark your child's creative imagination, such as *Once Upon a Time . . .* (#42) or *Make Up a Space Story* (#112).

Peppa and George love this book. We hope you do, too! Snort! Snort!

Contents

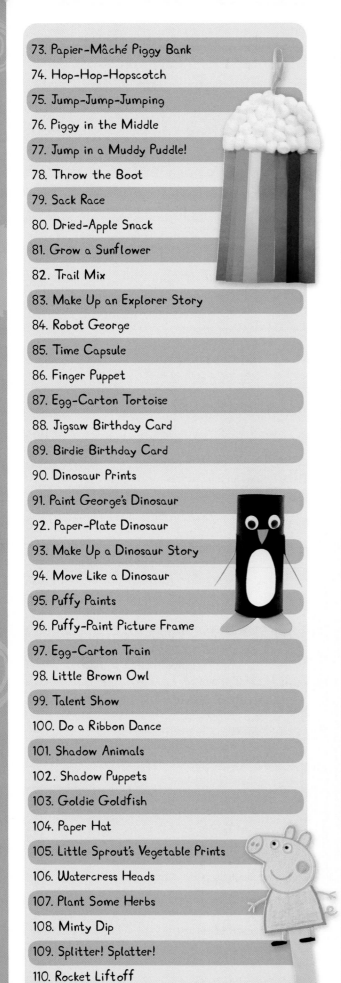

1 Peppa's House

Build a house like Peppa's, with a red tiled roof and yellow walls.

You will need:
* Square cardboard box, with flaps
* Cardboard
* Masking tape
* Pencil
* Scissors
* White, blue, and red poster board
* Glue
* Paintbrush
* Poster or acrylic paints
* Black pipe cleaners or toothpicks

1

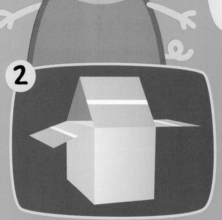

Cut four pieces of cardboard, the same size and shape as the box's flaps.

2

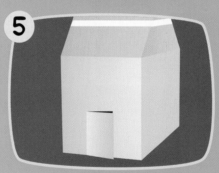

Stick the poster board to the flaps. Tape the two longer flaps together to make the roof.

3

Hold the smaller flaps up and draw along the shape of the roof on each flap.

4

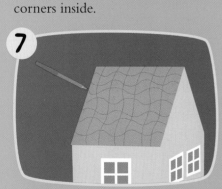

Fold along the pencil lines toward the roof and push the corners inside.

5

Cut out a front door, leaving one side attached so the door can open and close.

6

Paint the house the same colors as Peppa's house, then glue on the windows.

7

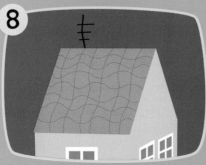

Glue sheets of red poster board to the sloped roof. Use red paint or a red pen to draw on the tiles.

8

Make an antenna out of black pipe cleaners or black-painted toothpicks glued together.

To make the windows:

Cut out squares of white poster board as shown. Cut out four squares in each to make the window frames. Glue a piece of blue poster board behind each window, then stick them to the side of the house.

Your pipe-cleaner or toothpick antenna can be pushed through and fixed in place with a blob of glue.

2 Peppa and George

Make a mini Peppa and a mini George to play in your house!

You will need:
* Poster board
* Scissors
* Paints or colored pencils
* Craft sticks
* Glue

templates

Copy or trace the templates onto the poster board. Cut them out, color them, then glue them onto craft sticks. Snort!

3 Peppa's Car

Beep! Beep! It's Peppa's little red car. Where are Peppa and her family going today?

You will need:
* Poster board
* Scissors
* Paints or colored pencils
* Craft stick
* Glue

Copy or trace the template onto the poster board. Cut it out, color it, then glue it onto a craft stick. Brrrm!

Beep! Beep!

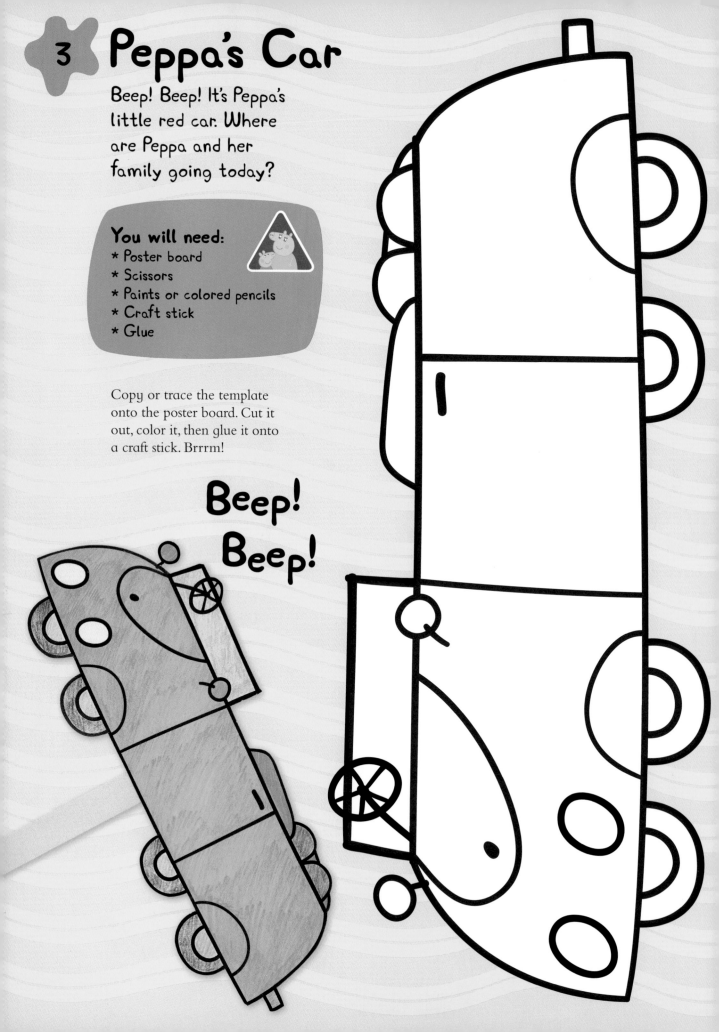

4 Peppa's Ears

Use the templates to make some pink Peppa ears. Snort! Hee hee!

You will need:
* Dark and light pink poster board
* Scissors
* Glue
* Pencil

1 Copy or trace the large ear templates onto dark pink poster board, then cut them out.

2 Cut two strips of poster board, 2 in x 12 in. Glue them together to make one long headband.

3 Measure the headband to fit around your little piggy's head, then glue or tape the ends together.

4 Copy or trace the smaller inner ear templates onto light pink poster board, then cut them out. Stick them on the main ear pieces.

5 Glue the two Peppa ears onto the middle of the headband. Snort!

Oink!

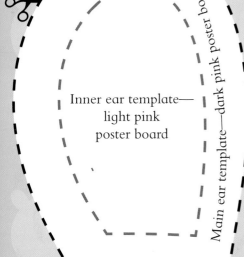

Inner ear template—light pink poster board

Main ear template—dark pink poster board

Inner ear template—light pink poster board

Main ear template—dark pink poster board

Hee! Hee!

Oink!

5 Grampy Rabbit's Submarine

Ahoy there! Grampy Rabbit's submarine is made out of bits of rubbish. You can make this one out of papier-mâché!

You will need:
* Sausage-shaped balloon
* Old newspaper
* Glue
* Water
* Large bowl
* Yogurt container
* Bendy straw
* Scissors
* Toothpick
* Plastic bottle
* Black and white paint
* Paintbrush
* Black poster board
* Safety pin
* Masking tape

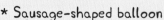

To make papier-mâché:
- Mix together one part glue and three parts water in a large bowl.
- Tear sheets of old newspaper into long thin strips, around 1 in wide x 2 in long.
- Soak the strips in the glue mix. Overlap the strips as you paste them onto your balloon.

1

Blow up a sausage-shaped balloon and cover it in 5–6 layers of papier-mâché. When it is dry, pop the balloon with a safety pin.

2

Ask an adult to make a hole with scissors in the base of a yogurt container and push the top of a bendy straw through the hole.

3

Use masking tape to stick the container to the top of your balloon. Cover the container and straw in 2–3 layers of papier-mâché.

4

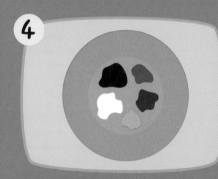

When all the papier-mâché is dry, mix together black and white paint to make different shades of gray.

5

Paint a patchwork design all over the submarine. Print rivets with the end of a paintbrush.

6

Cut a propeller from the side of a plastic bottle, and stick it to the end of a toothpick.

propeller cut from the side of a plastic bottle

toothpick

7

Glue on a porthole cut from black poster board, and push in the toothpick propeller at one end.

Peppa's Theater

Make a theater from a shoebox. Then put on your very own play!

1

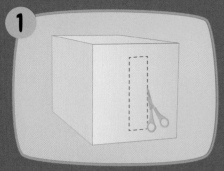

Cut openings at the sides of the box so the puppets can slide inside.

2

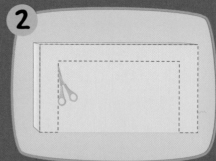

Cut a large rectangle in the shoebox lid to make the frame around the stage. Glue the lid to the shoebox on three sides and leave to dry.

3

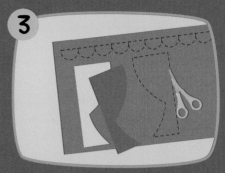

Cut curtains and frills out of red poster board to fit the front of the theater.

4

Add lines in black felt-tip pen to look like gathers in the curtains.

5

Glue the curtains and frills to the top and sides of the shoebox.

6

Paint the frame gold. When dry, paint glue in swirls around the edges and add gold glitter.

7

Cut some plain paper to fit the back of the box. Then draw and color a background.

8

Glue or tape the background picture to the back of the theater.

9

Cut tree shapes out of green poster board and stick them to the background.

Turn the page to find out how to make actors for your shoebox theater!

7 Put on a Play

Make puppets and put on Peppa's school play in your shoebox theater. (See #6 for instructions.)

You will need:
* Shoebox theater
* Cardboard
* Scissors
* Colored pens or pencils
* Craft sticks
* Glue
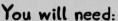

1 Copy or trace the templates below onto cardboard and cut them out.

2 Color the cardboard characters to match the ones in the pictures on the next page.

3 Glue each of the puppets to the end of a long craft stick.

templates

Little Red Riding Hood

The Big Bad Wolf locks Little Red Riding Hood's grandma in a cupboard. He jumps into Grandma's bed and pretends to be her so he can eat Little Red Riding Hood! Use these lines to make up your own version of the play.

Little Red Riding Hood: You don't look like my grandma!
What big eyes you have!
What big teeth you have!
You are NOT my grandma!
You are the BIG BAD WOLF!

The Big Bad Wolf: I am going to eat you up! Grrrr!

Little Red Riding Hood: Help! Help!

The Hunter: Go away, you naughty wolf.
I have saved you, Grandma!

Grandma: Thank you for saving me!

8 Fairy Wings

These pretty fairy wings are made from layers of tissue paper sprinkled with glitter and stars.

You will need:
* Cellophane
* 8-10 sheets tissue paper
* Diluted glue (1 part glue, 3 parts water)
* Paintbrush
* Glitter
* Tiny hearts and stars stickers
* Scissors
* Cardboard
* Hole punch
* Two 16-inch lengths elastic
* Construction paper

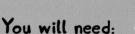

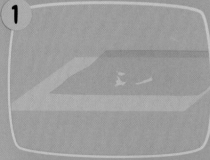

1

Lay a sheet of tissue paper over a piece of cellophane.

2

Brush the glue mixture over the paper. Lay another sheet of tissue on top.

3

Add the rest of the tissue paper, in layers, brushing the glue mixture between each layer.

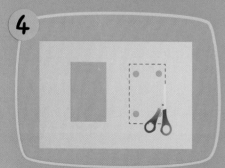

4

Cut two pieces of cardboard 2 in x 3 in. Make holes in each long side of one of the pieces with a hole punch, as shown.

5

Thread one piece of elastic through the top and bottom holes on the left side.

6

Knot the ends together, then do the same on the right with the other piece of elastic.

7

When it's dry, peel the hardened tissue paper off the cellophane.

8

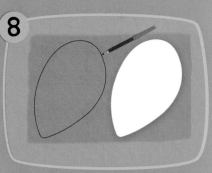

Draw a teardrop shape on a sheet of construction paper and cut it out. Use this as a template for tracing around on the tissue paper, and then cut out two shapes for the wings.

9

Glue the wings onto the poster board in the center, overlapping the pointed ends in the middle. Glue the second piece of poster board in the middle on the other side to hide the ends of the wings under the poster board.

10

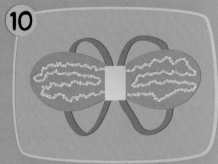

Brush glue on the top of the wings and the poster board, then sprinkle with glitter and tiny hearts and stars.

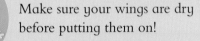

Make sure your wings are dry before putting them on!

9 Wand

Swish! Swish! Make a wish with this pretty fairy wand.

Use the template to cut two star shapes out of cardboard. Cover a wooden chopstick or craft stick and the star shapes with aluminum foil. Glue or tape the two stars together around the end of the stick. Decorate with scrunched-up tissue paper and a shiny stick-on jewel.

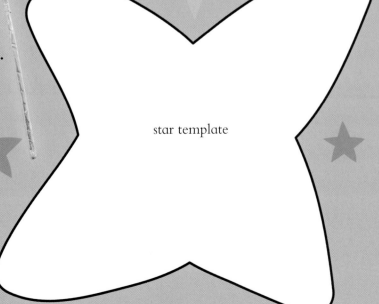

star template

10 Frilly Fairy Skirt

Peppa loves parties! This year she's going to have a fancy-dress birthday party and dress up as a fairy princess. Here's how to make a fairy-princess costume so you can look just like Peppa!

You will need:
* White or pink ribbon or elastic
* Colored netting
* Scissors
* Needle and thread (if using elastic)

1 Ask a grown-up to cut the elastic or ribbon to fit around your waist, plus an extra 10-12 in for the bow if using ribbon.

2 Measure the netting into strips of fabric twice the length of your skirt. For example, if you'd like your skirt to be 12 in long, your strips need to be 24 in long.

3 Ask an adult to help you cut 20 strips. The thicker you cut the strips, the fluffier your skirt will be!

4
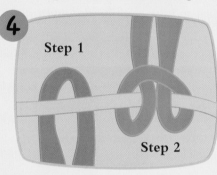
Step 1

Step 2

Fold your strip in half to create a loop at the top. Place the strip under the ribbon or elastic, so that the loop sticks out at the top, and pull the ends through the loop. Pull the knot tight.

5 Add more strips. Wrap the skirt around your waist, and tie the ribbon in a bow. If you have used elastic, ask a grown-up to sew the ends together.

11 Fairy Princess Tiara

Use the template to make a glittery tiara fit for a fairy princess.

1 Trace the tiara template onto the back of the glitter poster board, then cut it out.

2 Cut a long strip of poster board with a width of 1-1/2 in to make the headband.

3 Glue or tape one end of the tiara and headband together.

4 Decorate with foam shapes and stick-on gems.

5 Measure the headband to fit around your head, then glue or tape the ends together.

Hold the pieces in place with paper clips while the glue dries.

stick-on gems

You will need:
* Glitter poster board
* Scissors
* Glue or tape
* Decorations, such as stick-on gems or foam shapes
* Paper clips

tiara template

Tooth Fairy Envelope

Place a baby tooth in this little envelope and see if the tooth fairy swaps it for a shiny coin!

template

Apply glue here

1

Apply glue here

2

3

You will need:
* Paper
* Glue
* Felt-tip pens
* Scissors

1 Trace or photocopy the template onto the paper.

2 Fold flaps 1 and 2 away from you.

3 Turn the envelope over and apply glue to tabs.

4 Fold flap 3 inward and stick it to the tabs. Decorate your envelope with pens.

5 Fold the final flap inward and pop your tooth inside before tucking the flap in, ready for the tooth fairy.

13 Pretty Fabric Bag

Turn a plain fabric tote into this pretty bag, decorated with hearts and flowers!

You will need:
* Ironed canvas tote bag
* Poster board
* Plain fabric
* Fabric glue
* Embroidery thread
* Needle
* Buttons
* Colored felt
* Pinking shears or scissors

1 Trace or copy the templates below onto the poster board and use them to cut the shapes out of fabric or felt. For fabric, use pinking shears so the edges do not fray. For felt, you can decorate the edges with a blanket stitch.

2 Arrange the hearts and flowers on the front of the bag, and glue them in position with fabric glue.

template

Sew on small buttons for the flower centers.

How to do blanket stitch:

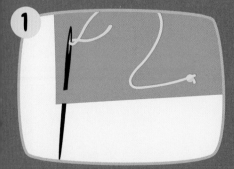

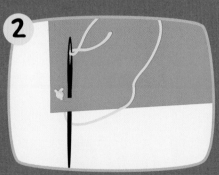

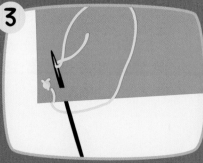

1 Knot the end of the thread and push the needle down through the fabric about 1/4 in away from the edge, then pull through.

2 Push the needle down through the fabric again just to the right of your first stitch. Pull the needle through the loop.

3 Push the needle down again through the fabric about 1/4 in to the right of your last hole and pull through the loop. Repeat this last step until you have stitched all the way around.

14 Fairy-Tale Castle

Here's how to make your very own fairy-tale castle!

You will need:
* 1 large cardboard box
* 4 smaller cardboard boxes (long)
* Scissors
* Glue
* Pencil
* Red and blue poster board
* Toothpicks
* Paints
* Paintbrush
* Silver and gold metallic pens

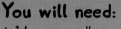

Who's going to live in your fairy-tale castle?

1

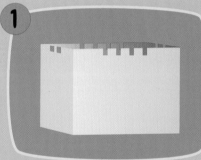

Cut the flaps off the top of the large box. Then cut squares in the top to look like battlements.

2

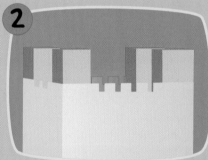

Glue one of the long, small boxes into each corner of the bigger box.

3

Cut little squares in the top of each tower. Draw an arched doorway on the front of the castle.

4

Paint the castle yellow. When dry, paint the entrance brown and add some arched windows.

5

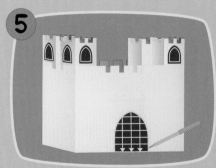

Use a silver metallic pen to draw lines over the brown doorway to make a portcullis.

6

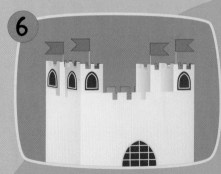

Make flags out of red poster board glued onto toothpicks, and add one to the top of each tower.

Paint green vines up the walls of the castle.

Make hanging flags to go around the sides using red and blue poster board. Draw on some crowns with a gold pen.

Fairy Cakes

These princess fairy cakes are delicious! Decorate them with cherries and pink frosting. Yum!

You will need:
* 7 tablespoons unsalted butter (softened)
* 1/2 cup granulated sugar
* 2 eggs, beaten
* 3/4 cups self-rising flour
* 1/2 teaspoon baking powder
* 12 cupcake liners
* Cupcake pan

To decorate:
* 16-ounce container vanilla frosting
* Food coloring (optional)
* 6 candied cherries, halved

1 Heat the oven to 400°F and fill a cupcake pan with 12 cupcake liners.

2 Beat together the sugar and butter (with a spoon or electric mixer) until the mixture turns pale and creamy.

3 Add the beaten eggs a little at a time.

4 Fold in the flour and baking powder.

5 Divide the mixture into the cupcake liners.

6 Bake for 15–20 minutes until golden brown, then leave to cool.

Open your container of frosting. If you like, add a drop of pink food coloring, and stir. Put half a candied cherry on top of each cupcake.

16 Time for Tea

Have a princess tea party for your friends. Serve princess fairy cakes on dainty plates and ask your friends to come dressed in their very best princess costumes.

17 The Princess and the Frog

Look! Her Royal Highness Princess Peppa is having a party at the palace. All the fairy princesses are having a lovely time, when suddenly a green frog hops out of the fountain.
"If you kiss a frog, it may turn into a handsome prince," says Princess Suzy Sheep.
"Yuck, I'm never kissing a frog!" says Princess Peppa.

Make up the rest of the story.
What happens next?

Valentine Cards

Make one of these cards for someone special on Valentine's Day!

You will need:
* Folded colored poster board
* Tissue paper
* Wrapping paper
* Glue
* Scissors
* Stick-on gems

Draw the outline of a large heart on the front of the poster board and glue on lots of tiny balls of scrunched-up tissue paper.

Cut heart shapes out of wrapping paper and glue them onto the front of a poster board on top of each other or in a row. Decorate with stick-on gems around the edges.

19 Valentine Heart

This pretty heart is made of felt and has a little ribbon so you can hang it up!

You will need:
* Poster board
* Pencil
* Felt
* Ribbon
* Cotton balls
* Embroidery thread
* Needle
* Fabric glue
* Scissors

1 Trace or copy the templates below onto poster board and use them to cut out felt heart shapes—two large, one medium, and one small.

2 Drizzle fabric glue around the edge of one large heart. Then glue the two large hearts together, leaving a gap at the top.

3 Glue the medium-sized heart and the small heart on the front of the large heart, and leave under a heavy book to dry.

4 Stuff the heart with cotton balls to pad out the shape. Glue a piece of folded ribbon in the gap at the top.

hanging ribbon

Decorate the edge of the heart with blanket stitch.

heart templates

See #13 for blanket stitch.

20 Friendship Bracelets

Peppa and Suzy Sheep are busy making friendship bracelets. Here's how you can make some, too.

You will need:
* ★ Embroidery thread
* ★ Masking tape
* ★ Scissors
* ★ Beads

1

Choose three lengths of different-colored thread. Knot the three ends together, then tape the knot to a tabletop.

2

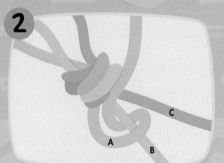

Hold thread B with your left hand. Loop thread A around B, then thread the end through the loop to make a knot.

3

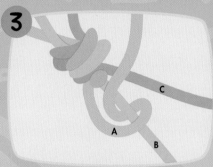

Pull the knot tight. Then repeat to make a second knot, so you have two knots on thread B.

4

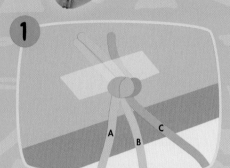

Hold thread C with your left hand. Loop thread A around C, then thread the end through the loop to make a knot.

5

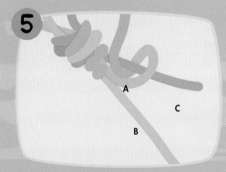

Pull the knot tight. Then repeat to make a second knot so you have two knots on thread C.

6

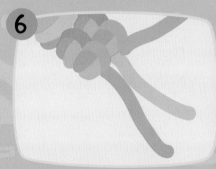

Start the next row, making knots from left to right, following the pattern in the panel at the top of the next page.

7

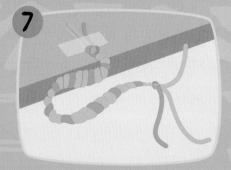

Keep knotting the threads until you have made a bracelet that is long enough to fit around your friend's wrist.

8

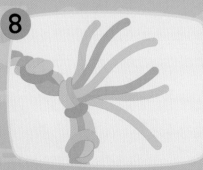

Trim the ends of the thread, making sure they are long enough to tie on the bracelet.

Thread some beads onto your bracelet as you make the knots.

Row 1:

Knot A twice onto B.
Knot A twice onto C.

Row 2:

Knot B twice onto C.
Knot B twice onto A.

Row 3:

Knot C twice onto A.
Knot C twice onto B.

21 Mummy Pig's Day Daffodil

Peppa is making Mummy Pig a pretty daffodil in a pot to say "Happy Mummy Pig's Day!"

You will need:
* Yellow and green poster boa▮
* Pencil
* Scissors
* Egg carton
* Colored tissue paper
* Glue
* Green straw
* Ribbons
* Modeling clay
* Flowerpot
* Paints
* Paintbrush

1 Copy or trace the daffodil templates onto bright yellow poster board. Cut out the flowers.

2 Tear a cup shape from an egg carton, paint it dark yellow or orange, and glue it to the main flower shape when dry.

3 Glue some scrunched-up tissue paper inside the egg-carton cup.

4 Tape the flower to the end of a green straw.

5 Draw some long daffodil leaves onto green poster board, cut them out, and glue them onto the stick.

6 Push the bottom of the stick into a lump of modeling clay and wedge it into a pretty pot.

daffodil template

daffodil template

Add scrunched-up tissue paper for soil in your pot, and tie pretty ribbons around it to decorate!

This daffodil makes a lovely Mother's Day present for your Mummy Pig!

22 Spring Flowers

Look for the first flowers of the year in your garden or the park. Can you spot any tiny white snowdrops or bright yellow daffodils?

23 Tulip Prints

Print a row of tulips to make a picture for your wall, a pretty birthday card, or some wrapping paper!

You will need:
* Potatoes
* Knife
* Acrylic or poster paints
* Bowls
* Poster board
* Cardboard
* Hole punch

1 Cut a potato in half, then cut away the flesh to leave a tulip shape.

2 Dip the potato into bowls of paint and print a row of colorful tulips onto poster board.

3 Print the green stems by dipping the edge of a piece of cardboard into green paint.

4 Print the leaves with the tips of your fingers—one print for each leaf!

hole made with hole punch

Printed tulips make pretty cards and gift tags!

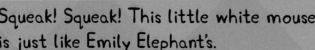

24 Emily Elephant's White Mouse

Squeak! Squeak! This little white mouse is just like Emily Elephant's.

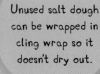

1

Roll and shape some salt dough into a mouse shape.

2

Cut a piece of string to make a tail. Make a slit in the bottom of the mouse's body and push the end of the string into it, covering it with dough to seal.

3

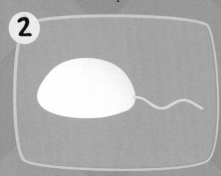

Shape the ears and eyes out of dough and attach them to the mouse's body with a little water. Use the end of a paintbrush to give the mouse a smile!

4 Bake, leave to cool, paint with acrylic paint, and then varnish with glue when dry. (See #46 for instructions.)

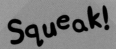

Squeak!

Unused salt dough can be wrapped in cling wrap so it doesn't dry out.

To make salt dough:
- Mix together 1/3 cup salt and 2 cups all-purpose flour in a mixing bowl.
- Slowly add 1 to 1-1/2 cups of lukewarm water and mix into a dough.
- Knead the dough for around 3–5 minutes until it is smooth.
- Bake models in the bottom of an oven (at 300°F) for around 3 hours, then leave to cool.

25 Chinese Lanterns

Make some pretty paper lanterns to hang up at Chinese New Year!

You will need:
* Colored construction paper
* Scissors
* Glue
* Metallic pen
* Shiny stickers or gems

Use glitter, gold stars, and shiny gems to decorate.

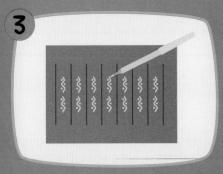

1

Cut a strip off the end of a sheet of paper to make the handle.

2

Fold the paper in half lengthwise, then make cuts across the fold. Leave about 1 in at the edge.

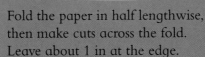

3

Draw a pattern on the lantern with a metallic pen, glue on strips of patterned paper, or add shiny stickers or gems.

4

Glue the edges together to make the lantern shape. Then glue the handle so the ends are inside the top of the lantern.

Pretty Easter Eggs

Here's how to make an egg carton full of pretty decorated Easter eggs!

You will need:
* 6 eggs
* Egg carton
* Glue
* Paintbrush
* Colored tissue paper
* Paints
* Poster board
* Ribbon
* Scissors

1. Crack an egg in half, pour out the insides, and wash it carefully. Glue the shell back together along the edges.

2. Cover the whole egg in glue, then add 3–4 layers of torn-up scraps of tissue paper.

3. When dry, paint a pretty pattern on the egg with paint.

4. Photocopy the pictures below and stick them onto some posterboard. Carefully cut them out and attach each one to some ribbon around the center of each egg.

5. Decorate your egg carton with scraps of tissue, or paint it.

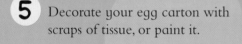

27 Easter Bunnies

Make some cute bouncy bunnies out of toilet-paper rolls.

You will need:
* Toilet-paper rolls
* Paint
* Paintbrush
* Poster board
* Glue
* Googly eyes
* Felt-tip pen
* Cotton balls
* Scissors

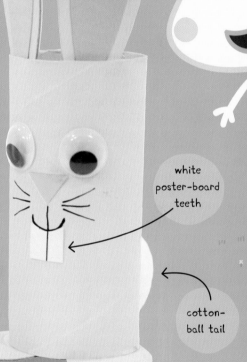

Cut out and stick different-colored poster board to the inside of the ears.

googly eyes

white poster-board teeth

cotton-ball tail

rabbit ears and feet template

1 Paint a toilet-paper roll any color you like.

2 Copy or trace the template onto poster board to make two long rabbit ears and two big feet, and cut them out. Paint the ears and feet to match the bunny's body, then glue them to the top and bottom of the roll.

3 Stick on two googly eyes. Cut a triangle out of pink poster board for the nose and a white rectangle for the teeth. Draw a mouth and whiskers with a felt-tip pen. Don't forget to give your bunny a cotton-ball tail!

28 Easter Bonnet

Peppa loves her Easter bonnet! Create your own beautiful bonnet by following these simple steps!

You will need:
* Straw hat
* Scissors
* Colored poster board
* Colored foam
* Colored tissue paper
* Glue
* 3 polystyrene eggs
* 32 inches of yellow ribbon

1

Cut the ribbon in half and stick or sew one piece to each side of the inside rim of the hat, to make the ties.

2

Cover each polystyrene egg in glue, then add 2–3 layers of torn-up scraps of tissue paper.

3

To make the flowers, trace the templates onto colored poster board and cut out the shapes.

4

Use your fingers to gently press each petal in one by one. This will give each flower a realistic shape and realistic dimensions.

5

Layer and glue your colored flower pieces together, using the different sizes and circles to form the centers.

6

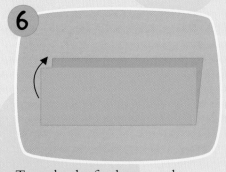

To make the feathers, cut the foam to 6 in x 8 in. Then fold in half lengthwise to make a long rectangle.

7

Cut the rectangle of foam into a semicircle shape, and then cut triangles out along the curved edge. Open the shape. Make two more feathers in different colors.

8

Once all the pieces are dry, arrange them on the hat and glue them in place.

29 Easter Basket

Make this little Easter basket to hold some tiny chocolate eggs.

You will need:
* Wrapping paper
* Pencil
* Ruler
* Scissors
* Glue
* Colored straw or shredded paper
* Chocolate eggs
* Colored poster board

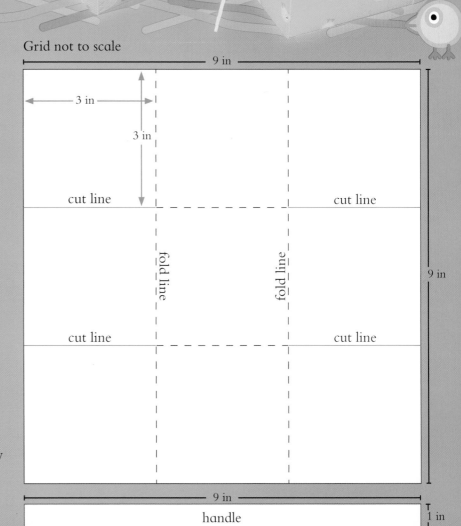

1 Measure and draw the grid 9 in x 9 in onto a piece of colored poster board.

2 Stick a sheet of wrapping paper on the other side—this will be the outside of the basket.

3 Cut the four lines, as marked, from the edges to the central square.

4 Fold the poster board in the center.

5 Overlap and glue together at the sides.

6 Cut out a handle of more wrapping-paper-lined poster board, and glue inside the basket.

7 Fill the basket with colored straw or shredded paper. Now you can pop in some tiny chocolate eggs—yummy!

Grid not to scale

9 in

3 in

3 in

3 in

cut line   cut line

fold line   fold line

cut line   cut line

9 in

9 in

handle

1 in

30 Easter Egg Hunt

Circle the Easter eggs that Mummy and Daddy Pig have hidden in the garden!

31 Egg Necklace

Peppa has hidden a toy inside her egg-shaped necklace. What are you going to hide in yours?

You will need:
* 2 eggs
* Newspaper
* Glue
* Water
* Scissors
* Paints
* Paintbrush
* Yarn or embroidery thread

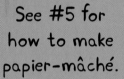

See #5 for how to make papier-mâché.

1

Hard-boil two eggs, cool, then cover 3/4 of each egg in 4–5 layers of papier-mâché. Leave to dry.

2

Remove the top of each egg. Scoop out the insides and shells, then cut a zigzag edge on each paper egg.

3

Paint the outside and the inside of the eggs. Make two holes next to each other in the top and bottom of each egg.

4

Braid three strands of yarn or thread into a chain.

5

Thread both ends of the chain through the top of one egg and out the bottom of the other. Knot the chain below the bottom egg and leave the ends loose.

Now your necklace is ready to fill and wear!

32 Rebecca Rabbit's Ears

Use the templates to make some Rebecca Rabbit ears.

1. Copy or trace the large ear template onto cream poster board twice, then cut them out.

2. Cut two strips of poster board, 2 in x 12 in. Glue the headband pieces together to make one long strip.

3. Measure the headband to fit, then glue or tape the ends together.

4. Copy or trace the inner ear template onto white poster board twice, then cut them out. Stick them onto the main ear pieces. Glue the two rabbit ears onto the middle of the headband. Squeak!

You will need:
* Cream and white poster board
* Scissors
* Glue or tape

Inner ear template— white poster board

Large ear template—cream poster board

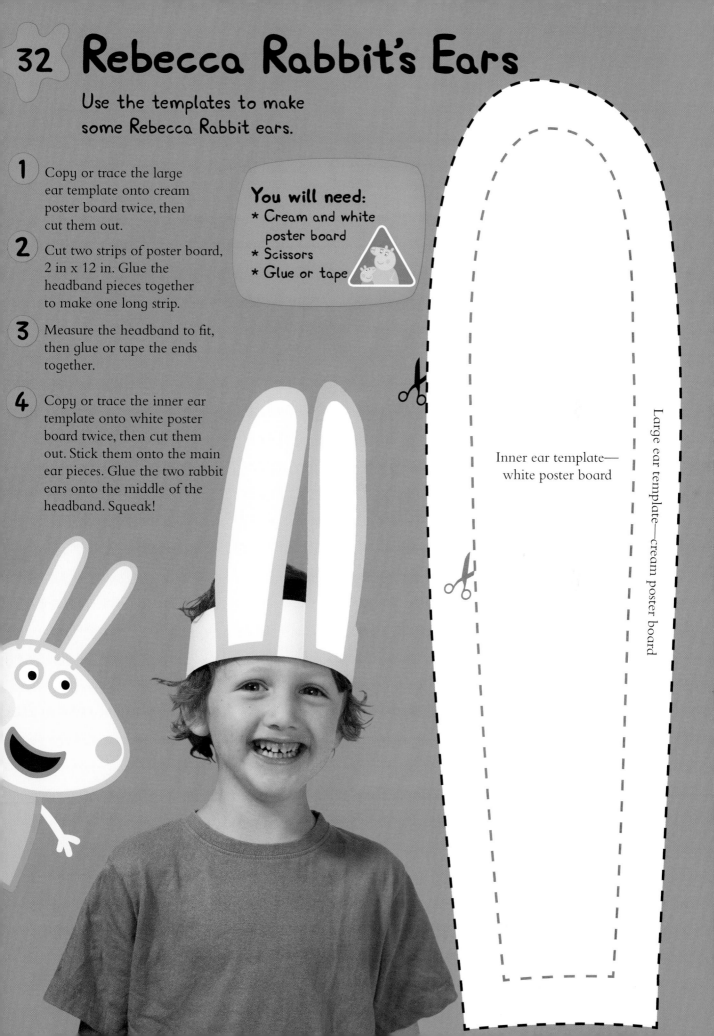

Miss Rabbit's Carrot Cake

Do you know Miss Rabbit's favorite cake? It's carrot, of course—with some tasty marzipan carrots on the top!

You will need:
* 1 cup self-rising flour
* 1 cup all-purpose flour
* 1 teaspoon baking soda
* 2 teaspoons ground cinnamon
* 1 teaspoon ground ginger
* 1 cup vegetable oil
* 1 cup soft packed brown sugar
* 4 eggs
* 3/4 cup golden syrup
* 3-2/3 cups grated carrot
* 1/2 cup pecans, chopped
* 5 tablespoons honey
* 9-inch round cake pan
* Parchment paper
* Toothpick

To decorate:
* 7 tablespoons unsalted butter, softened
* 2 teaspoons orange extract
* 2/3 cup cream cheese
* 1 cup powdered sugar
* Marzipan
* Orange and green food coloring

Delicious!

1. Preheat the oven to 320°F. Lightly grease the cake pan and line it with parchment paper.

2. Sift together the self-rising flour, all-purpose flour, baking soda, cinnamon, and ginger in a bowl.

3. Whisk the oil, sugar, eggs, and syrup in another bowl. Add to the flour mixture and stir well.

4. Stir in the grated carrot and nuts, spoon mixture into the cake pan, then bake for 1-1/4 to 1-1/2 hours until golden.

5. Remove the cake from the oven and make lots of little holes in the top with a toothpick.

6. Drizzle over the honey, then leave the cake to cool in the pan while you make the frosting.

7. Beat together the butter, orange extract, and cream cheese, then mix in the powdered sugar.

8. Remove the cake from the pan, slice it in half, and add a layer of frosting. Put some more frosting on top.

9. Color most of your marzipan orange with 1–2 drops of orange food coloring, then roll it into carrot shapes. Color the rest of the marzipan green to make the leaves. Add two long green leaves on each carrot. Munch! Munch! Very tasty!

Rebecca Rabbit likes carrot cake, too!

34 Indoor Den

When it's cold outside, have fun making an indoor den. Drape blankets and sheets over furniture, and fill your den with cushions and blankets.

35 Memory Game

One person chooses 8-10 everyday things (such as a teaspoon, a pencil, or a tiny toy) and arranges them on a tray. Everyone then has 30 seconds to look at the things on the tray before they are covered up. Who can remember the most things?

36 Treasure Hunt

Get someone like Mummy Pig or Daddy Pig to hide some treasure, then have fun looking for it! The treasure could be a chocolate coin or a small toy.

IN THE HALL
Above the boots, below the hat is where you'll find this clue is at!

IN THE KITCHEN
Find a dish that's red and blue, and look . . . you'll see another clue!

Make it more difficult by having clues—one clue leads to another clue, and then that clue leads to another clue—so it takes longer to find the treasure.

37 Muddy Puddles Game
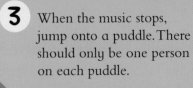

Splat! Here's a muddy puddles game you can play indoors!

1 Cut some big puddle shapes out of thick brown cardboard and attach them to the floor with reusable adhesive. There should be one puddle fewer than the number of players.

2 Dance around the puddles while some music is playing.

3 When the music stops, jump onto a puddle. There should only be one person on each puddle.

4 The player who doesn't jump onto a puddle in time is out of the game. Remove a puddle and start again.

5 The winner is the first person to jump onto the last puddle when the music stops.

Jumping in muddy puddles is Peppa's favorite thing to do!

38 Balloon Race

Have a balloon race! Each person puts a balloon between their knees and races across the room. How fast can you go without dropping the balloon?

39 Balloon Bounce

Blow up some balloons. How long can you keep tapping your balloon to keep it in the air? Who can keep their balloon in the air the longest?

40 Knight's Helmet

Look! It's Brave Sir George! Here's how to make a helmet fit for a fairy-tale knight.

You will need:
* Cardboard
* Poster board
* Scissors
* Masking tape
* Aluminum foil
* Feathers (red and yellow)
* Paper fasteners
* Tape

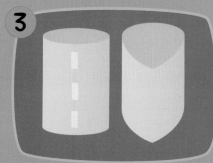

1 Cut out a piece of cardboard wide enough to fit around your head and long enough to reach from above your head to your shoulders. Cut a large square from the center of the cardboard for your face.

2 Taking a piece of poster board, cut out a grille shape slightly larger than the square hole, with slits to see through. Cover it in aluminum foil.

3 Roll the large piece of cardboard into a cylinder shape, and tape the ends together. Make a fold down the opposite side of the helmet to the tape so the front of the helmet comes out into a point.

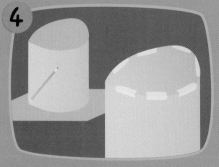

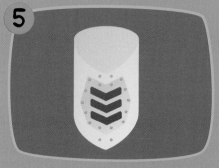

4 Cut out a teardrop-shaped piece of cardboard to fit the top of the helmet. Cover the helmet and the teardrop shape in foil, then tape them together.

5 Attach the grille over the outside of the hole with a row of paper fasteners to look like rivets. Bend back the arms of the paper fasteners inside the helmet.

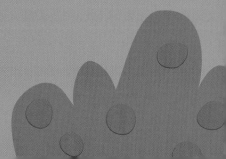

Brave Sir George's Shield

If Brave Sir George is going to chase away the scary green dragon, he'll need a shield! Here's how to make one.

You will need:
* Scissors
* Glue
* Thick corrugated cardboard
* Poster board
* Masking tape
* Ruler
* Pencil
* Paints
* Paintbrush

Put your arm through the handle at the back of the shield to hold the shield in front of your body.

1

Cut two shield-shaped pieces of corrugated cardboard.

2

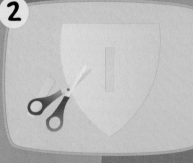

Cut a slit measuring 6 in x 1 in in the center of one piece of cardboard.

3

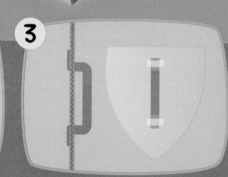

Cut a strip of poster board measuring 12 in x 1 in. Push the poster board through the slot and tape down the edges, as shown.

4

Glue the two parts of the shield together so the cardboard handle is sticking out the back on the outside.

5

Cover the rough edges around the outside of the shield with masking tape, then paint the whole shield yellow.

6

When dry, divide the shield into quarters with a ruler and pencil, then paint the two opposite quarters red.

Once Upon a Time . . .

Look! Her Royal Highness Princess Peppa is having
a picnic in the clouds with Brave Sir George. Oh no!
What's that terrible roar? It's a scary green dragon. . . .

Make up an exciting story about
what happens when Peppa and
George come face to face with
the scary green dragon!

43 Hubble Bubble

Here's how to make your own mixture to make lots and lots of bubbles.

You will need:
* Large bowl
* Dish soap
* Bottle of glycerin (from pharmacy, optional)
* Water
* Wire coat hanger

1 Mix together equal amounts of dish soap, water, and glycerin, if you have it.

2 Pour the mixture into a deep, wide bowl.

3 Ask an adult to bend a wire coat hanger into a circle. Dip it in the bubble mixture and wave it around!

Peppa and George LOVE blowing bubbles! How big is the biggest bubble you can blow?

Glycerin is not essential, but it will make your bubbles stronger!

44 Bubble Paintings

If you like blowing bubbles, why not print some colorful bubble patterns!

You will need:
* Large bowl
* Dish soap
* Water
* Paint
* Straws
* Plain white paper

1

Mix paints, water, and a squirt of dish soap in a bowl.

2

Blow air into the mixture through a straw to make lots of bubbles.

3

Gently rest a sheet of plain paper on top to make a bubble print.

45 Salt-Dough Beads

These pretty salt-dough beads can be strung into a bracelet or a necklace.

You will need:
* Salt dough
* Wooden skewers
* Poster paints
* Glue
* Water
* Ribbon
* Varnish

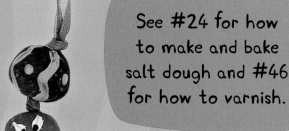

Thread beads onto a long piece of ribbon.

See #24 for how to make and bake salt dough and #46 for how to varnish.

Tie knots between the beads if you don't want them to move.

1 Roll the salt dough into a long sausage, then break it into smaller chunks so the beads are roughly the same size.

2 Roll each piece of dough into a ball between your palms.

3 Gently push a wooden skewer through the beads to make holes big enough to push ribbon or thread through. Make sure the holes are quite large, as the dough may spread slightly in cooking.

4 Remove the skewers and bake the beads until the dough has gone hard.

5 When cool, paint the beads with brightly colored poster paints, then varnish them.

You will need about 20 beads to make one necklace.

Mini Bug Bookmarks

Glue tiny balls of salt dough onto ribbons to make these colorful bug bookmarks!

You will need:
* Salt dough
* Paints
* Paintbrush
* Green ribbon
* Glue
* Water
* Pinking shears
* White tissue paper

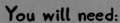

1 Model bugs out of salt dough, then bake following the instructions in #24.

2 Paint the bugs bright colors, then glue them onto the ends of long green ribbons.

3 Cut the ends of the ribbons with pinking shears so they don't fray.

If you varnish your bug bookmarks, they will last longer!

Layer white tissue paper with glue. Once dry, cut out some wings.

Salt-dough varnish:
- Mix one part glue to three parts water.
- Cover each model with the mixture when the paint is dry. (The mixture looks milky at first but dries clear and hard.)

47 Pom-Pom Chick

You can make lots of different animals when you know how to make a pom-pom. Here's how to make a little yellow chick.

You will need:
* Poster board
* Scissors
* Ruler
* Compass
* Pencil
* Yellow yarn
* Googly eyes
* Yellow and orange felt
* Glue

Cut out yellow felt wings and glue them on.

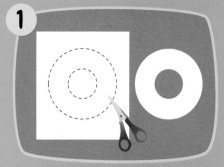

1 Fold a piece of poster board in half. Draw a 3-inch-wide circle with a 2-inch circle inside it.

2 Cut out both the large circles and the inner circles to make two donut shapes.

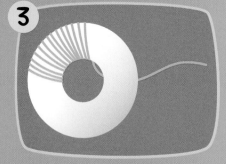

3 Put the two circles together. Wrap yarn around them until a tiny hole is left in the center.

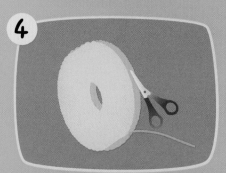

4 Snip the yarn around the edge. Keep snipping until you reach the poster board circles inside.

5 Tie a length of yarn between the pieces of poster board and knot it, to keep the yarn together.

6 Remove the poster board, trim the yarn into a neat ball, then cut out and glue on orange felt pieces for the beak and feet, and add googly eyes.

48 Pom-Pom Ice Cream

Turn some pom-poms into these tasty-looking ice cream cones.

You will need:
* Brown poster board
* Pencil
* Scissors
* Large plate
* Various colors of yarn
* Glue

1 Follow steps 1–5 on the opposite page to make a pom-pom. Use a different color of yarn for each flavor.

2 Remove the poster-board circles and trim the yarn into a neat ball.

3 Place the plate on the poster board and trace it. Cut out the circle.

4 Fold the circle in half, then in half again, then cut along the folds.

5 Take one of the quarter circles and curve it into a cone shape. Glue it in place, then pop an ice cream pom-pom on top!

Peppa's Ice Cream

open

Strawberry

Vanilla

Chocolate

49 Pirate Card

Shiver me timbers! This birthday card is perfect for anyone who loves pirates!

You will need:
* Colored poster board
* White poster board for stencil
* Scissors
* Paints
* Sponge

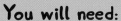

1 Copy or trace the skull-and-crossbones template onto poster board and cut it out.

2 Hold the stencil over a piece of poster board and dab paint through it with a sponge.

3 Let the paint dry before writing your card.

Happy Birthday, Danny Dog!

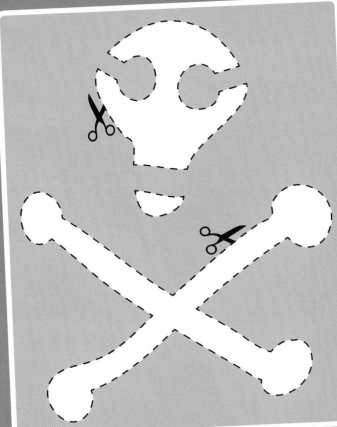

Danny Dog's Pirate Hat

Ho, ho, me hearties! Danny Dog is having a pirate party. Here's how to make a pirate hat like Danny Dog's.

You will need:
* 16-1/2 in x 23-1/2 in black construction paper
* Tape or glue
* Pirate stencil
* White poster paint
* Sponge

A-harrr!

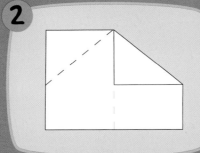

Dab white paint over the pirate stencil with a sponge to add this scary skull and crossbones on the front of the hat.

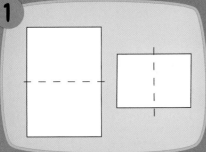

1

Fold a piece of black paper in half, then in half again. Open out the second fold.

2

Fold down the top corners, as shown, then fold them back the opposite way.

3

Open out the paper slightly, then push the corners down and inside the folds.

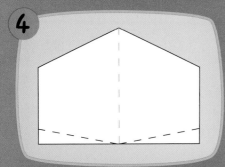

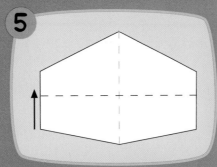

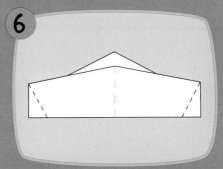

4

Fold the bottom edges up at each side, as shown. Turn over and repeat the same folds on the other side to match.

5

Fold the paper up at the front. Turn over and repeat on the back to match.

6

Fold back the corners at each side of the hat on the front and back. Tuck the folds inside and glue or tape them together.

51 Treasure Cup

This gleaming golden cup makes perfect pirate treasure!

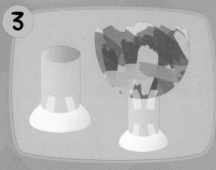

You will need:

* Oval balloon
* Newspaper
* Glue
* Water
* Poster board
* Scissors
* Compass
* Pencil
* Toilet-paper roll
* String
* Gold or silver paint
* Paintbrush
* Stick-on gems
* Tape
* Safety pin

1

Blow up a balloon and cover half of it in 5–6 layers of papier-mâché. Pop the balloon with a safety pin when dry.

2

Cut out a circle of poster board, make a slit from the edge to the center, and tape it into a cone shape.

3

Push the cone inside a toilet-paper roll and tape the roll to the bottom of the papier-mâché bowl.

4

Make sure the cup can stand up, then cover the base in 3–4 layers of papier-mâché.

5

Cut out two strips of poster board and tape them to the sides of the bowl to make handles. Cover in papier-mâché.

6

Trim the top of the bowl with scissors and glue strips of paper over the edge to neaten it.

7 Glue string around the stem and bowl of the treasure cup to make a raised pattern.

8 When the glue is dry, paint the cup silver or gold, and add some shiny stick-on gems.

See #5 for how to make papier-mâché.

52 Paper Boat

Make a boat from a sheet of paper!

1

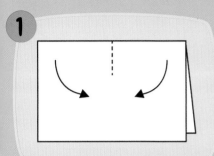

Fold the paper in half, then make a crease in the center, at the top.

2

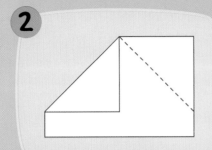

Fold down each corner toward the middle.

3

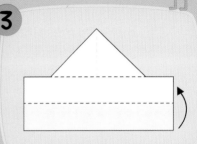

Fold the edges of the paper up on both sides, then open out the paper in a hat shape.

4

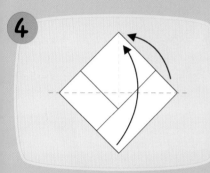

Bring the corners of the hat toward each other and flatten the shape into a square.

5

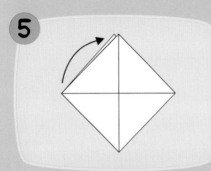

Hold the open corners of the square and fold each one up to make flattened triangles, as shown in the drawing in step 6.

6

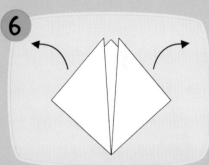

Flatten the triangle into a square by opening it up in the middle to fold the two bottom corners together and fold flat into a square.

7

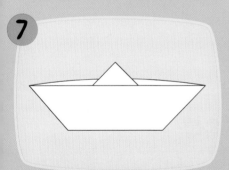

Gently pull the sides of the triangle out to make a boat shape.

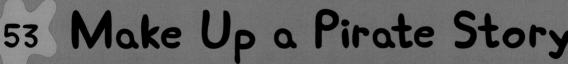

53 Make Up a Pirate Story

Shiver me timbers! Captain George and Pirate Peppa have followed a treasure map all the way to a desert island. They start to dig in the sand for buried treasure, when suddenly some more pirates arrive. . . . Make up a story about what happens next.

54 Treasure Map

Why not make a secret treasure map showing where you plan to bury some pirate treasure?

55 Treasure-Map Case

Next, make this case to keep your treasure map safe!

You will need:
* Long canister with a lid
* Brown poster board
* Paper fasteners
* Rope or thick string
* Glue
* Black tape or poster board
* Scissors

1

Wrap and glue brown poster board around the canister and cut out a circle to stick on the lid.

2

Glue a long piece of thick string to the sides of the canister at the top.

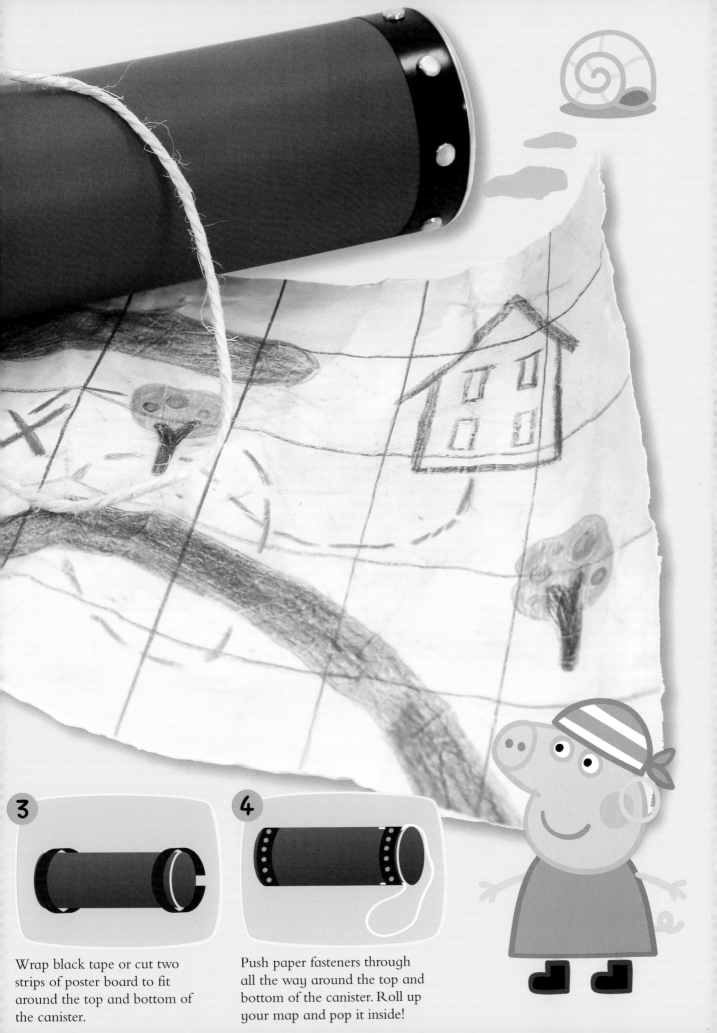

3 Wrap black tape or cut two strips of poster board to fit around the top and bottom of the canister.

4 Push paper fasteners through all the way around the top and bottom of the canister. Roll up your map and pop it inside!

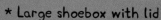

56 Treasure Chest

Every pirate needs a chest to store his or her treasure in. . . .

You will need:
* Large shoebox with lid
* Brown poster board
* Pencil
* Glue
* Brown and black paints
* Paintbrush
* Old comb or brush
* Black tape or poster board
* Gold poster board
* Paper fasteners
* Plate
* Scissors

Add black poster board straps studded with paper fasteners.

1

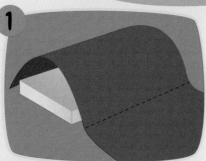

Cut a piece of brown poster board long enough to curve over the top of your shoebox lid to make a dome shape.

2

Trace a plate that's the same width as the shoebox lid onto another piece of paper. Then draw a bigger circle (1 in wider) around the first circle. Cut around the bigger circle, then cut it in half.

3

Snip around the edges of the semicircles to the inner line, then fold the flaps over. Glue the semicircles to either side of the lid along the flat edges.

4

Glue the long piece of brown poster board over the top, curving the poster board and sticking it to the flaps on both sides as you go along.

5

Cover the base of the shoebox in brown poster board. Drag black paint into lines with the teeth of an old comb to make the paper look like wood.

6

Cut a keyhole shape out of black poster board and stick it onto a square piece of gold poster board. Glue it onto the front of the shoebox.

Captain Peppa Says . . .

Decide who is going to be Captain Peppa and play this simple game with your shipmates!

Captain Peppa tells all the other players what to do, but they must only do things that start with the command "Captain Peppa says . . ."

If Captain Peppa says "Captain Peppa says touch your toes!", you must do it.

But if she only says "Touch your toes!" and you do it, you will be out of the game.

Mr. Potato

Make your very own Mr. Potato!

1 Choose a big potato to be your Mr. Potato.

2 Use the template to make his hat from felt and glue the felt pieces onto a piece of poster board to make it sturdy.

3 Poke cloves into the potato to make Mr. Potato's eyes and use the templates to make his smiley mouth and mustache from poster board, then stick them on.

You will need:
* Big potato
* Scissors
* Black and red poster board
* Brown and yellow felt
* Glue
* Cloves
* Pipe cleaners

Push in pipe cleaners for his hands and feet.

Now make Mr. Potato's car on the next page!

hat template

mustache and mouth templates

Mr. Potato's Car

Mr. Potato has come to town! Make his car from papier-mâché and an empty plastic bottle.

You will need:
* Sausage-shaped balloon
* Newspaper
* Glue
* Water
* Large plastic soda bottle
* Scissors
* Cardboard (red, yellow, and black)
* Poster paint
* Paintbrush
* Toothpicks
* Safety pin

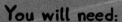

1

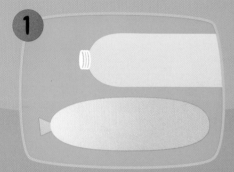

Blow up a sausage-shaped balloon so it's the same width as the bottle.

2

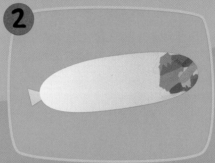

Cover the rounded end of the balloon with 3–4 layers of papier-mâché.

3

Use lots of papier-mâché to build up the sides to form the car shape.

4

Pop the balloon with a safety pin when the glue is dry. Cut the edge and glue strips of paper over it to make it neat.

5

Leave the car to dry, then paint it red. Glue on four black cardboard wheels, a stripy grille, and two yellow headlights.

6

Copying the shape in the picture opposite, cut out a red rotor and fix it into the top of the bottle with a toothpick.

Cut a round steering wheel out of black cardboard and stick it to a toothpick. Glue the toothpick to the front of the car so Mr. Potato can steer!

Slide the bottle carefully over Mr. Potato so he's ready to drive away!

See #5 for how to make papier-mâché.

60 Sun Wall Hanging

Make this bright yellow sun to hang on your wall!

What you need:
* Salt dough
* Large and small plates
* Rolling pin
* Water
* Paintbrush
* Blunt knife
* Pencil
* Small metal hook
* Paint
* Varnish

1

Roll out some salt dough, then ask an adult to help you cut around a large plate to make a circle.

2

Roll out some more salt dough, then cut around a small plate to make a smaller circle.

3

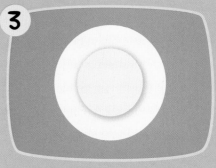

Wet one side of the small circle with water and stick it to the middle of the large circle.

4

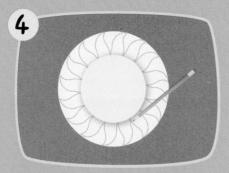

Make the shape of the sun's rays in the dough with a pencil and ask an adult to cut them out.

5

Bake your sun in the oven. Leave to cool, then paint it in bright sunshine colors. Attach the metal hook to the back of your sun to hang it on the wall.

See #24 for how to make and bake salt dough and #46 for the varnish.

61 Rainmaker

Tip this instrument from side to side to make a swooshing sound like falling rain!

You will need:

* Long cardboard canister with a lid
* Aluminum foil
* Dried rice, lentils, or peas
* Craft foam or cardboard
* Colored or white paper
* Paints
* Paintbrush
* Scissors
* Glue
* Decorations

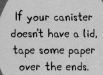

1 Gather and twist a sheet of aluminum foil into a spiral and put it inside the canister.

2 Fill the canister a quarter full of dried rice, lentils, or peas, then put on the lid.

3 Cover your canister in colored or white paper, then paint your rainmaker bright colors. Glue on some craft foam shapes, glittery sequins, or craft feathers.

If your canister doesn't have a lid, tape some paper over the ends.

Remove some foil if the rice or peas get stuck, or add more if they move down the canister too fast and you want to slow them down.

Tip or shake the instrument to hear the swooshing sound.

A Rainy-Day Walk

Put on your raincoat and some rain boots,
then go for a walk in the rain.
Have fun splashing in all the puddles!

See how many of these things you
can find on your walk in the rain:

* Gray clouds
* Slugs or snails
* A wiggly worm
* A muddy puddle
* A rainbow

63 Weather Watch

What's the weather like today? Make a weather chart to see how the weather changes where you live.

You will need:
* Large sheet of paper
* Felt-tip pens or colored pencils
* Ruler

1 Divide the paper into boxes, one for every day of the week or month.

2 Write the days of the week along the top of the calendar.

3 Make up some little pictures to show all the different kinds of weather . . .

4 . . . then draw a picture to show what the weather is like every day!

Monday	Tuesday	Wednesday	Thursday	Friday	Saturday	Sunday
1	2	3	4	5	6	7
8	9	10	11	12	13	14
15	16	17	18	19	20	21
22	23	24	25	26	27	28
29	30	31				

Peppa likes rainy days because then you get MUDDY PUDDLES! Snort!

64 Rainbow and Clouds

Make this hanging cloud and rainbow to remind you of your rainy-day walk!

You will need:
* Paper plate
* Cotton balls
* Glue
* Paintbrush
* Tissue paper in all the colors of the rainbow!
* Ribbon

1 Fold the paper plate in half and glue it together.

2 Paint on glue with a brush and cover the plate with cotton balls to make a cloud.

3 Cut strips of tissue paper in various colors so they are all the same length, and glue them onto the back of the plate.

4 Stick a loop of ribbon to the top of the cloud to hang up your rainbow.

Put the strips in order so they match the colors of the rainbow.
The order is:
* red
* orange
* yellow
* green
* blue
* indigo
* violet

65 Shadow Tag

On a sunny day, try to "tag" someone by stepping on his or her shadow.

The person chasing everyone else's shadows is "it." If he or she steps on someone's shadow, then that person becomes "it" instead!

Hot-Air Balloon

Up, up and away! Make this colorful hot-air balloon to hang from your ceiling!

1

Blow up an oval balloon and cover three quarters of it in 5-6 layers of papier-mâché. When dry, pop the balloon with a safety pin and remove it.

2

Cut a large yogurt container in half. Tape the top half of the yogurt container to the balloon, as shown, and cover both parts of the container in 3–4 layers of papier-mâché.

3

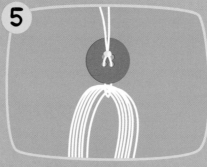

Divide the balloon into 12 sections and paint them different colors. Paint the other half of the yogurt container to look like a basket.

4

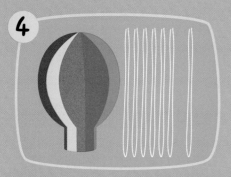

Measure a piece of string from the top of the balloon to the bottom and then double it. Cut seven pieces of string this length.

5

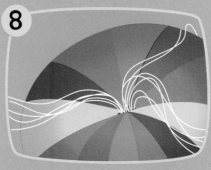

Place six of the strings together and fold them in half. Tie the seventh piece of string around the halfway point. Thread the button onto the tied string and knot it in place.

6

Have an adult cut a tiny slit at the very top of the balloon using a craft knife. The slit should just be big enough to push the edge of the button through.

7

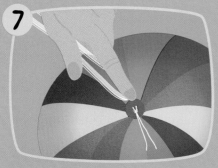

Holding all of the strands, slide the button into the slit so it twists into place and can't be pulled out.

8

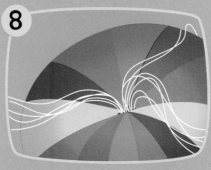

Hold the two strands attached to the button together to keep them out of the way. These will be the hanging strings for your balloon when finished.

9

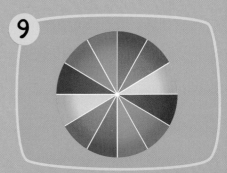

Carefully position each of the other strands equally around the balloon to divide the color sections.

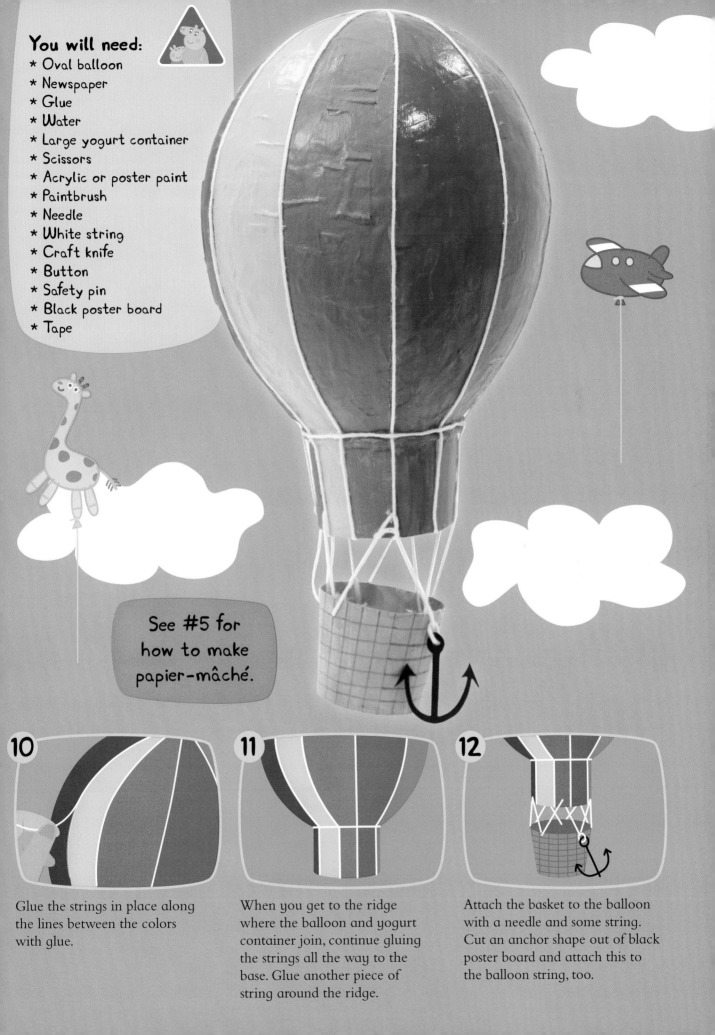

You will need:
* Oval balloon
* Newspaper
* Glue
* Water
* Large yogurt container
* Scissors
* Acrylic or poster paint
* Paintbrush
* Needle
* White string
* Craft knife
* Button
* Safety pin
* Black poster board
* Tape

See #5 for how to make papier-mâché.

10

Glue the strings in place along the lines between the colors with glue.

11

When you get to the ridge where the balloon and yogurt container join, continue gluing the strings all the way to the base. Glue another piece of string around the ridge.

12

Attach the basket to the balloon with a needle and some string. Cut an anchor shape out of black poster board and attach this to the balloon string, too.

67 Fridge Magnets

These little cars and trains have magnets on the back so you can stick them on the front of your fridge!

You will need:
* Salt dough
* Paints
* Glue
* Water
* Tiny magnets
* Varnish

Shape cars, trucks, and trains out of salt dough. Bake the models and leave to cool. Paint in bright colors and glue a tiny magnet onto the back of each model.

Paint on a coat of glue mixed with water to "varnish" the models (see #46).

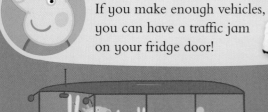

Peppa says . . .

If you make enough vehicles, you can have a traffic jam on your fridge door!

See #24 for how to make and bake salt dough.

68 Printing Fun

Have fun printing using all sorts of everyday things found around the house.

You will need:
* Paper
* Bowls of thick paint
* Corks
* Glue
* Objects to print with

Try printing with:
- Buttons
- Coins
- Dried pasta shapes
- Wooden paintbrush ends
- Old keys
- Cookie cutters

Glue buttons and other small objects onto corks or small pieces of wood to make them easier to print with. Dip them into the bowls of paint to make prints on the paper.

69 Fingerprint Flowers

You can also print with your fingers! Paint this lovely flower with your fingertips.

You will need:
* Plain paper
* Colored paper
* Paints
* Corrugated cardboard
* Glue
* Scissors
* Your fingers!

Print the stem with the edge of a piece of corrugated cardboard dipped in paint. Make the flowers by printing lots of colorful dots in circles with the tip of your finger.

Cut a vase shape out of colored paper and glue it over the stems.

70 Fingerprint Animals

Make lots of little animal prints using your fingers and thumbs!

Buzzy bees
Dip your thumb in yellow paint and press it onto a piece of paper to paint the body. When dry, draw on stripes, legs and wings with a black felt-tip pen. Then draw on an eye or glue on a tiny googly eye instead.

Ants
Make three black blobs with different-sized fingers. Draw on antennae and legs when the paint is dry and glue on a googly eye.

Frogs
Make a green blob with your thumb or fingertip. When the paint is dry, draw on a mouth and legs, and glue on two googly eyes.

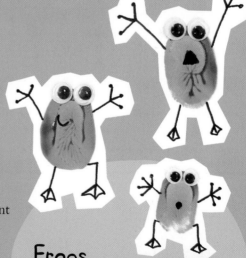

Peppa's Photo Album

Here's Peppa's photo album, full of pictures of her family and friends. Why not make one, too?

1

Cut out two equal-sized pieces of cardboard. Glue them on the back of your sheet of wrapping paper, leaving a narrow gap between them.

2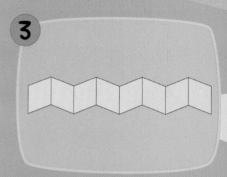

Cut around the wrapping paper so it is 1 in bigger than the cardboard. Fold down the edges of the paper and glue them onto the cardboard.

3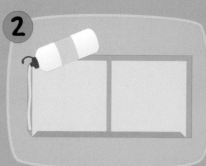

Tape together lots of sheets of paper and fold them into an accordion to make your photo album's pages. (See the next page for how to make an accordion.)

4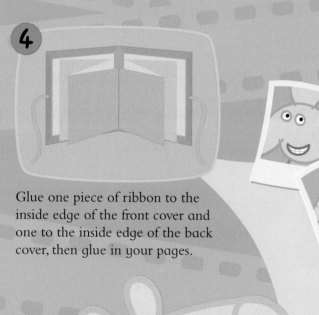

Glue one piece of ribbon to the inside edge of the front cover and one to the inside edge of the back cover, then glue in your pages.

You will need:
* Scissors
* Colored cardboard
* Brightly colored wrapping paper
* Glue
* Tape
* Plain or colored paper
* Two lengths of ribbon
* Stick-on gems
* Photographs!

Use stick-on gems, rolled-up swirls of paper, pictures, or anything else you like to decorate the front cover. Now you are ready to stick your photos inside!

See #2 for a Peppa template to trace and color for your cover.

George   Suzy Sheep   dfish

To make an accordion:

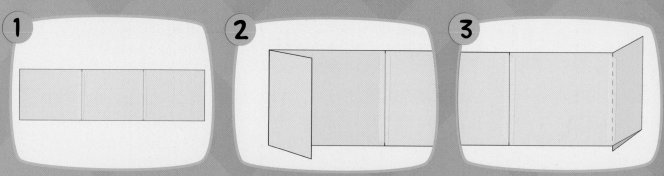

1 Tape some sheets of paper together to make one long strip of paper.

2 Fold the edge of the paper over, to the size you want your book page to be.

3 Turn the strip of paper over and fold the paper back on top of the first fold.

4 Repeat turning the paper over and folding it until you have a long accordion.

Sweet Dishes

These little sweet dishes are made out of papier-mâché covered in layers of colorful tissue paper.

You will need:
* Plate
* Cling wrap
* Old newspaper
* Glue
* Water
* Scissors
* Tissue paper

1

Wrap a piece of cling wrap over a plate. (This will stop the papier-mâché from sticking.)

2

Cover the front of the plate with four layers of papier-mâché, then leave to dry.

3

Peel your dry paper dish off the plate, then cut around the edge to neaten.

4

Cover both sides of your dish in strips of brightly colored tissue paper. Glue on 3–4 layers of tissue paper so you cannot see the newspaper underneath.

See #5 for how to make papier-mâché.

73 Papier-Mâché Piggy Bank

Save your pennies in this papier-mâché piggy bank!

You will need:
* Oval or round balloon
* Newspaper
* Glue
* Water
* Poster board
* Masking tape
* Pipe cleaner
* Scissors
* Poster paint
* Paintbrush
* Yogurt container
* Pin

1

Blow up the balloon, and cover it in five layers of papier-mâché, leaving a small area around the knot uncovered. Then leave to dry.

2

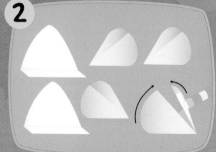

Cut two ear shapes from poster board. Cut two circles of poster board in half, then glue into cones to make the legs.

3

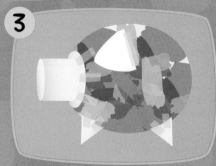

Ask an adult to use a safety pin to pop and remove the balloon. Then tape the legs, ears, and yogurt-container snout onto your pig's body.

4

Ask an adult to make a hole in the back with a pin. Push in a curly pipe-cleaner tail.

5

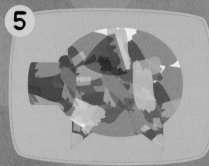

Cover the ears, legs, snout, and tail with two layers of papier-mâché, and leave to dry.

6

Ask an adult to cut a slit in the top for your pennies, then paint your papier-mâché piggy!

Make sure the papier-mâché is completely dry before painting—this can take 2–3 days!

74 Hop-Hop-Hopscotch

Peppa and her friends love playing hopscotch. Using chalk, draw a grid on a safe driveway, pavement, or in a playground to play.

You will need:
* Chalk
* Small, smooth pebbles
* Your hopping and jumping skills!

Make each box about 12 in square.

1 Using chalk, draw your hopscotch grid, copying the picture above. Then take turns throwing your pebbles onto the squares.

2 To start, throw your pebble into square 1. Jump over the stone, landing with both feet on squares 2 and 3. Then hop onto square 4 and jump with both feet on squares 5 and 6. Next, hop onto square 7, jump with both feet on squares 8 and 9, then hop onto square 10.

3 Hop around to face the opposite way, then jump and hop back, picking up your pebble from square 1 as you go.

4 Next, throw your pebble so it lands inside square 2 and continue jumping and hopping up and down the hopscotch grid.

5 Miss a turn if you don't throw your stone into the correct square, or if you step on a chalk line.

75 Jump-Jump-Jumping

Find a jump rope and see how many jumps you can do in one turn. Can you get to 10 or 20 or even more?

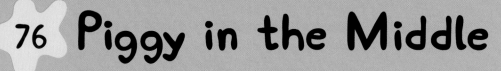

76 Piggy in the Middle

To play Piggy in the Middle, two people throw a ball to each other while someone in the middle tries to catch it. If the piggy in the middle catches the ball, then the person who threw it becomes the next piggy in the middle.

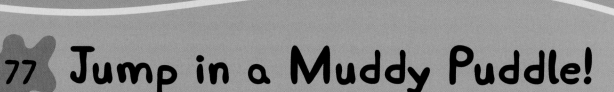

77 Jump in a Muddy Puddle!

Everyone loves to jump in muddy puddles! Put on your rubber boots and jump in muddy puddles, just like Peppa and George!

78 Throw the Boot

Take turns throwing the boot into a circle. You could use hoops or draw chalk circles on the ground. Write numbers inside the circles. Add up the points as you go around the course. The player with the most points wins!

79 Sack Race

Find some old pillowcases or sacks and have a sack race. Each person steps inside their pillowcase or sack, holds it up with their hands, and jumps! Who'll be the first to jump past the finish line?

80 Dried-Apple Snack

Dried apples make a healthy snack—they're very tasty, too!

You will need:
* Apples
* Apple corer
* Knife
* Lemon juice
* Water
* Baking sheet

1 Ask an adult to peel some apples, remove the cores with an apple corer, and thinly slice.

2 Soak the apple rings in water with a squeeze of lemon juice to stop them from turning brown, then pat them dry.

3 Arrange the apple rings on a baking sheet and cook in a low oven (around 150°F) for 5–6 hours, turning once, until the apples are dry and golden.

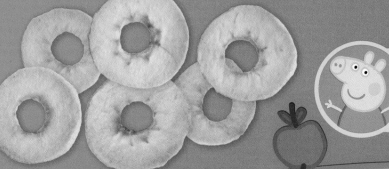

If you like the taste, you can sprinkle your apple slices with cinnamon before they go into the oven.

81 Grow a Sunflower

Grow a sunflower in your garden or in a large pot on a balcony.

You will need:
* Packet of sunflower seeds
* Patch of flowerbed or a large flowerpot and some potting soil
* Bamboo cane
* Garden twine
* Pencil

1 Put a bamboo cane in a flowerbed or large pot filled with potting soil. Make a hole in the soil with a pencil.

2 Put 2–3 seeds in the hole and cover them with soil.

3 Water the soil and wait for your sunflowers to grow.

4 As each plant grows, tie its stem to the bamboo cane with garden twine.

Harvesting your sunflower seeds

Sunflower seeds are ready to harvest when the backs of the flowers turn yellowy brown and start to droop.

Cut off the flowers and hang them up to dry or put them in a paper bag. Once dry, the seeds will fall out of the flower head. If your sunflower has edible seeds, wash the seeds before you eat them.

If you like, you can roast your sunflower seeds by spreading them on a baking sheet and placing it in the oven for around 45 minutes at 275°F. Stir the seeds occasionally as they cook.

Store the seeds in an airtight container.

Choose easy-to-grow sunflowers with seeds you can eat.

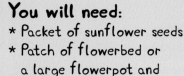

82 Trail Mix

Make a tasty trail mix to munch on next time you go for a walk!

Mix cupfuls of your favorite ingredients in a big bowl. Store the mixture in an airtight container until your next walk, then divide the trail mix into paper bags, one for each person. You could even add the dried apples from the previous page to the mix!

Here are some things to try:
- Sunflower seeds
- Unsalted nuts, such as hazelnuts or peanuts
- Raisins
- Chocolate chips
- Dried banana chips
- Dried coconut chips

83 Make Up an Explorer Story

Peppa and George are going for a walk in the woods to search for bugs and other animals.

"I hope I find some ants," says Peppa. George wants to see a bee. Make up a story about all the different creatures Peppa and George find in the woods.

84 Robot George

Look at George dressed as a robot! Here's how to make a robot costume, too.

You will need:
* Large cardboard box
* Small cardboard box
* Scissors
* Aluminum foil
* Colored poster board
* Plastic bottle caps
* Glue
* 2 green pipe cleaners
* Black yarn

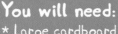

1 Check the boxes to make sure there are no staples or sharp edges inside.

2 Remove or tape up any loose flaps.

3

Try the large box on for size, then ask a grown-up to cut armholes for you in each side and a square at the top for your head to go through. Then cut a large square in the front of the small box so you can see out of it.

4

Glue shiny aluminum foil all over the boxes and decorate with glued-on bottle caps and shapes cut out of colored poster board.

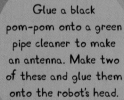

Glue a black pom-pom onto a green pipe cleaner to make an antenna. Make two of these and glue them onto the robot's head.

See #47 for how to make a pom-pom.

85 Time Capsule

Fill a metal box with things about you and your family, then hide it somewhere safe.

Tape the lid shut and write a message on the lid that your time capsule is not to be opened for 5, 10, or even 15 years!

Things to include:
* Photographs
* Drawings
* Birthday cards
* Tickets to a favorite place
* A little toy
* Favorite jokes
* Songs recorded on a memory stick

Hide your time capsule in a safe place, but don't forget where you put it! Hee Hee!

Finger Puppet

Here's how to make a little poster board finger puppet that looks just like Candy Cat's tiger!

You will need:
* Poster board
* Scissors
* Tape or glue
* Colored pens or pencils

1 Copy or trace the templates onto poster board, then color them.

2 Roll the body shape into a cone. Tape or glue along the edge.

3 Cut out the head and tail, and glue onto the cone.

templates

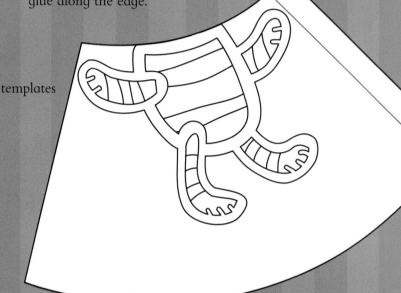

Meow!

Color in the stripes.

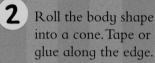
Give Candy Cat's tiger a smiley face!

Egg-Carton Tortoise

This little egg-carton tortoise looks just like Dr. Hamster's Tiddles!

You will need:
* Poster board
* Scissors
* Cardboard egg carton
* Glue
* Paint
* Paintbrush
* Googly eyes

1 Copy or trace the template onto green poster board or plain poster board painted green, and cut out.

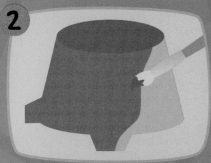

2

Tear out the compartment of a cardboard egg carton and paint it pale brown.

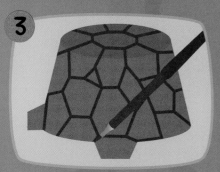

3

When dry, paint dark lines on the egg carton to match Tiddles's shell.

4

Glue the shell onto the body. Then stick on the eyes and give Tiddles a smiling red mouth.

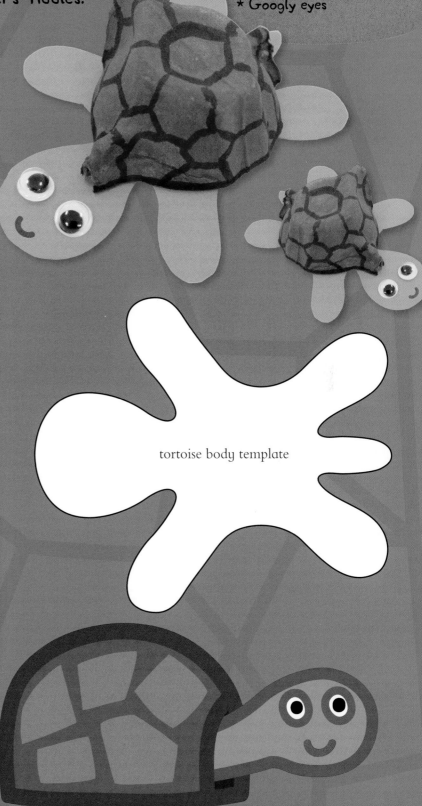

tortoise body template

Jigsaw Birthday Card

Peppa is making a jigsaw birthday card for Suzy Sheep's birthday!

You will need:
* Cardboard
* Paints or colored pencils
* Paintbrush
* Black felt-tip pen
* Ruler
* Pencil
* Scissors
* Envelope

1 Cut the cardboard into a square measuring 6 in x 6 in.

2 Draw or paint a colorful picture on one side of the cardboard.

3 Draw the outline of a flower, heart, or star in black felt-tip pen on the other side of the card. Write your birthday message inside the black outline.

4 Using a ruler and pencil, divide the cardboard into 9 squares, each measuring 2 in x 2 in, then cut along the lines.

Your friend will have to put the puzzle together to read your birthday message!

Put the jigsaw pieces in an envelope.

Happy Birthday! Love from Peppa X

89 Birdie Birthday Card

This birthday card has a surprise inside—a birdie with a pop-up beak!

You will need:

* Orange, yellow, and pink poster board
* Scissors
* Glue
* Googly eyes
* Feathers
* Felt-tip pens

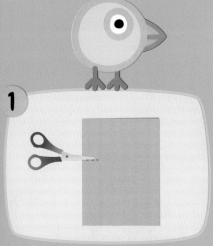

1

Fold a piece of orange poster board in half and cut a slit across the fold, as shown.

2

Fold back the flaps, then push the folded flaps inside your poster board to make the beak.

3

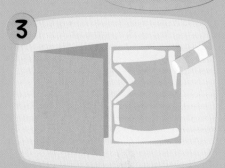

Glue a pink piece of poster board (the same size as the orange piece) behind the orange poster board, taking care not to stick it to the beak.

4

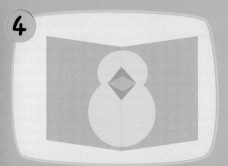

Cut out a curved shape from yellow poster board for the bird's head and body. Ask an adult to cut a diamond shape to fit the beak through. Stick inside the card.

Glue on some googly eyes and bright, colorful feathers!

Don't glue the pink poster board behind the beak or the chick's mouth won't open!

Decorate the front of the card with the words "Happy Birthday!" or any design you like!

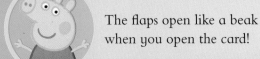

The flaps open like a beak when you open the card!

90 Dinosaur Prints

Here's how to make some roaringly good dinosaur wrapping paper and matching gift tags.

1 Use the templates to cut the dinosaur figure shape and the dinosaur footprint shapes out of craft foam.

2 Glue the shapes onto corks or small blocks of wood or boxes to make them easier to print with.

3 Brush paint onto the foam shapes, then press down onto the paper to make each print.

4 Cut out some of your dinosaur prints and glue them onto pieces of cardboard to make gift tags.

You will need:
* Cardboard
* Scissors
* Craft foam
* Glue
* Corks, wooden blocks, or small boxes
* Poster paint
* Paintbrush
* Brown wrapping paper
* Hole punch
* Ribbon

footprint template

dinosaur template

Make a hole in the top of the gift tag with a hole punch and thread through some ribbon.

91 Paint George's Dinosaur

Would you like to paint a green dinosaur like George's?

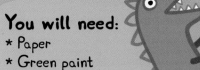

You will need:
* Paper
* Green paint
* Paintbrush
* Googly eyes
* Glue

---

1 First paint a big C-shape on your paper, like this:

2 Paint two straight lines going in from the ends, for the dinosaur's wide-open mouth.

3 Paint a long curved line to make the dinosaur's back and tail.

---

4 Then draw a curved line for the dinosaur's tummy. Make sure the lines meet in a point, to make the dinosaur's tail.

5 Paint two little arms . . .

6 . . . and legs.

---

7 Next, color in your outline with green paint.

8 Add blobs of paint down the dinosaur's back to make it look spiky.

9 Last of all, glue on two googly eyes.

Grrr!

Paper-Plate Dinosaur

Grrrr! This paper-plate dinosaur also looks like George's green dinosaur!

You will need:
* Paper plate
* Scissors
* Green paint
* Paper fasteners
* Felt-tip pens

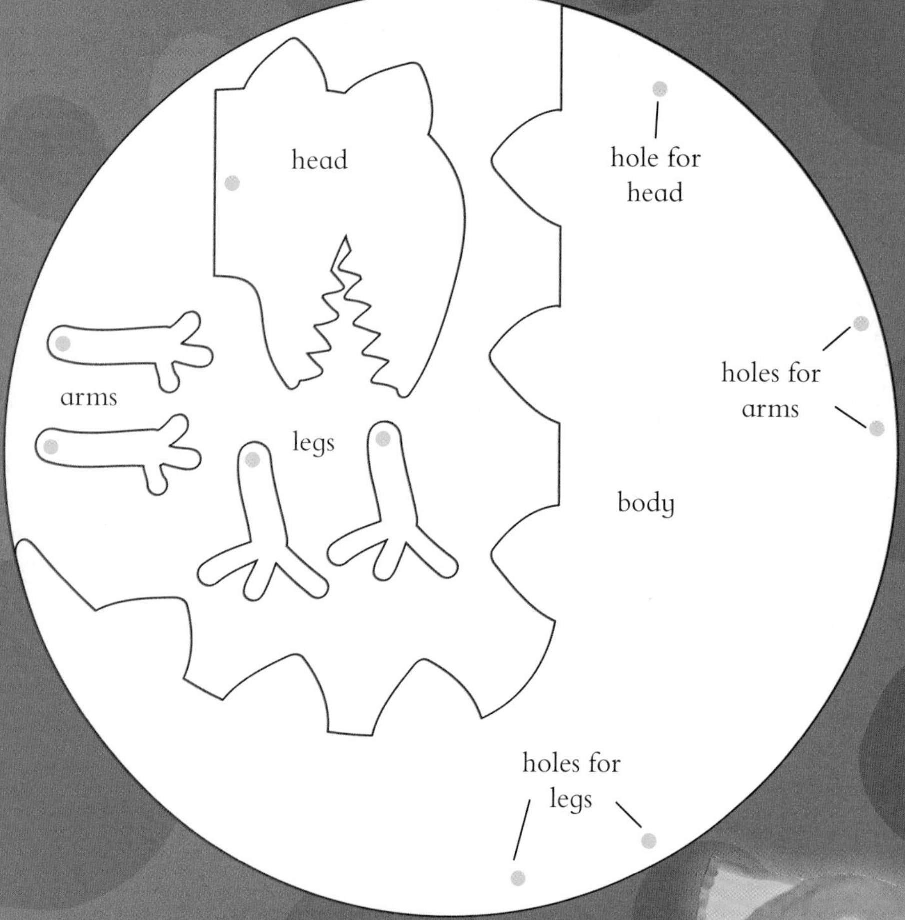

head

hole for head

arms

legs

holes for arms

body

holes for legs

1 Ask an adult to cut the pieces of the dinosaur's body out of a paper plate, as shown here.

2 Paint the dinosaur green, except for his eyes and teeth! Draw these on with felt-tip pens.

3 Fasten the pieces together with paper fasteners, as shown below.

Dine-saw!

93 Make Up a Dinosaur Story

Peppa and George have traveled back in time to the land of the dinosaurs. Everything is very quiet when suddenly some dinosaurs appear! ROOOOAAR! Make up a story about what happens next. . . .

94 Move Like a Dinosaur

Some dinosaurs stood on two legs, some walked on four, some flew, and some swam. Pretend to be a dinosaur and stomp and roar!

95 Puffy Paints

Make some puffy paints, then use them to paint a puffy-paint picture!

You will need:
* 1 cup flour
* 1 cup water
* 1 cup salt
* Selection of different food colorings
* Squeeze bottles

1 Mix together the flour, water, and salt with a few drops of food coloring. Put the mixture into a squeeze bottle.

2 Make up lots of bottles of puffy paint—use a different one for each color!

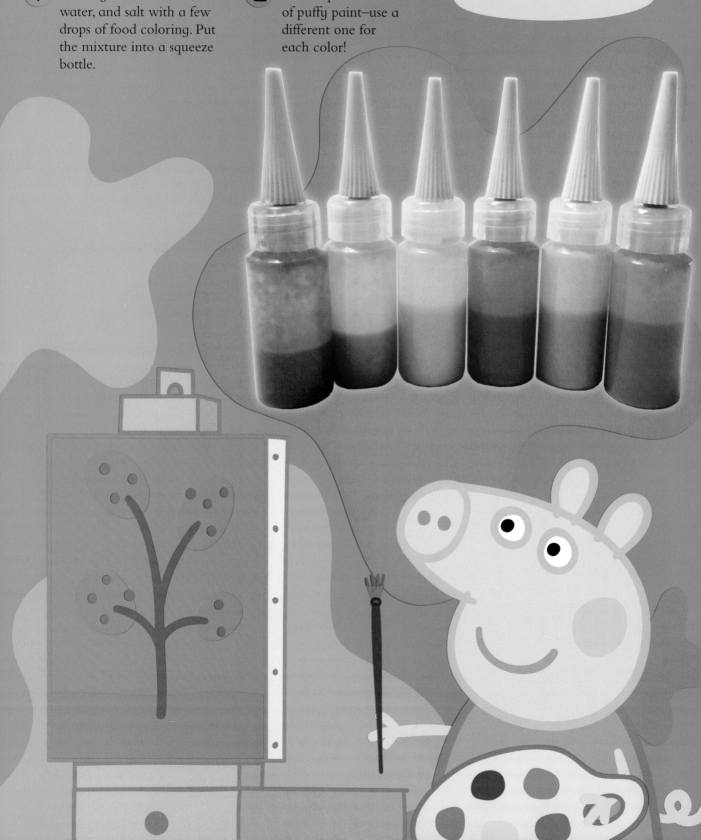

96 Puffy-Paint Picture Frame

Here's how to make a picture frame decorated with your homemade puffy paints.

You will need:
* Thick cardboard
* Scissors
* Ruler
* Pencil
* Glue
* Colored paint
* Paintbrush
* Puffy paints (See #95)

1. Cut out two pieces of thick cardboard, the size you want your picture frame to be.

2. Cut a window in one piece of cardboard.

3. Glue the front of the frame to the back, leaving one side open so you can slide in a photograph.

4. Paint the front and back of the frame with colored paint.

When dry, squeeze puffy-paint shapes and squiggles onto your frame.

Once the puffy-paint decorations are dry, slide your photograph into the frame.

Egg-Carton Train

Toot! Toot! This little egg-carton train looks like Grandpa Pig's train, Gertrude.

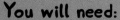

You will need:

* 2 toilet-paper rolls
* Scissors
* Masking tape
* Pipe cleaners
* Newspaper
* Glue
* Water
* White and colored poster board
* Cardboard egg carton
* Acrylic paints
* Paintbrush
* Tissue paper
* Bottle cap
* Penny
* Pencil
* Darning needle

1

Cut one toilet-paper roll in half and tape it to the top of the other roll to make the large funnel.

2

Scrunch up tissue paper to make the smaller funnel and tape in place.

3

Trace the end of the engine roll on some poster board, cut out the circle, and tape it to the front end of the engine roll.

4

Copy the shape shown for the back of the engine onto poster board, cut it out, and secure it to the back of the engine roll with tape.

5

Cover the engine in papier-mâché and leave to dry.

6

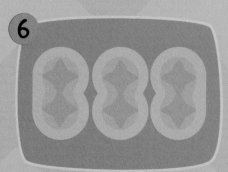

To make the carriages, cut the lid off the egg carton and then carefully cut the base of the egg carton into three pieces. Trim the longer edges so they're level with the other sides.

7 Once the papier-mâché on the engine has dried, paint it white and leave it to dry.

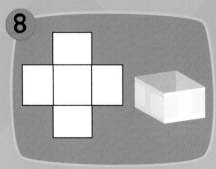

8 Copy the shape shown above onto poster board to make the driver's carriage. Fold and tape the sides together to make a box.

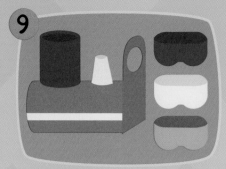

9 Paint the engine, driver's carriage, and egg-carton carriages to look like Gertrude and leave to dry.

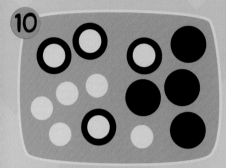

10 Trace a bottle cap on black poster board and cut out lots of wheels. Trace a penny on gray poster board, cut the circles out, and stick them in the middle of the black circles to make the wheels' centers.

11 Glue the driver's carriage onto the back of the engine.

12 Make holes with a darning needle and thread the pipe cleaners through to join the carriages together. Glue on the wheels to finish.

See #5 for how to make papier-mâché.

98 Little Brown Owl

Suzy Sheep loves her toy owl! Here's how to make a little toy owl.

You will need:
* Felt, craft foam, or poster board
* Scissors
* Black buttons
* Glue
* Ribbon
* Tape

1 Copy or trace the templates onto poster board, then use them to cut pieces out of foam, felt, or colored poster board.

2 Glue the pieces together as shown below, then tape a loop of ribbon behind the owl's head so you can hang it up.

Stick on two black buttons to complete the owl's eyes.

templates

99 Talent Show

Put on a talent show for your family and friends.

Peppa is very good at dancing, drawing, and acting in plays!

Your talent could be playing a musical instrument . . .

telling a joke . . .

reading a poem . . .

singing a song . . .

showing everyone a picture you have drawn . . .

or doing a cartwheel!

What's your talent?

100 Do a Ribbon Dance

Hold the ends of two pieces of wide, silky ribbon. What patterns can you make with the ribbon as you dance?

Shadow Animals

Peppa and her friends are having fun making shadow animals on the wall. Here are some shadow animals for you to try.

Shine a light onto a white wall. Make shadows by holding your hands between the light and the wall.

Open and close your hands to make your bird fly!

Bird
Cross your hands with your palms facing you and lock your thumbs together.

Swan
Bend one arm at the elbow and close your hand to make the head. Make the wing with your other hand.

Spider
Cross your hands with your palms facing you. Lock your thumbs and tuck them down to make the spider's head, then wriggle your fingers so they look like the spider's legs.

Snail
Make one hand into a fist and rest it on the back of the other, outstretched hand.

Shadow Puppets

If you like making shadow animals, put on a play using these shadow puppets!

templates

Make up a story as you move your shadow puppets around!

Trace or copy the templates onto cardboard, and cut them out. Then glue them onto craft sticks or long wooden chopsticks. Shine a light onto a wall and hold up the puppets so they cast a shadow.

103 Goldie Goldfish

Make this picture to show Peppa's pet goldfish, Goldie, swimming in her fish bowl!

You will need:
* Blue paper
* Paint
* Your fingers!
* Felt-tip pen

1 Print Goldie's body with your thumb dipped into orange paint. Print the tail with the tip of your finger.

2 When the paint is dry, draw on two eyes and a mouth.

3 Print some bubbles with your little finger dipped in white paint.

Don't forget to give Goldie a smiley mouth!

104 Paper Hat

All you need to make this paper hat is a big sheet of newspaper!

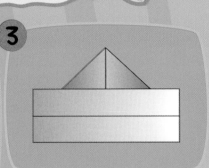

1

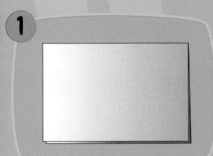

Fold the sheet of newspaper in half, then turn it around so the folded edge is at the top.

2

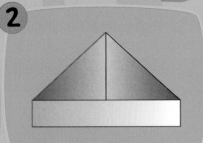

Fold down both of the top corners to the center, so they meet in the middle.

3

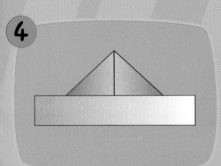

Turn up about 4 in of the bottom of one side of the newspaper, over the triangles.

4

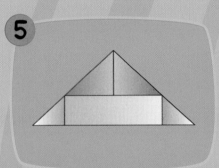

Flip over the paper and turn up the bottom edge on the other side, to match.

5

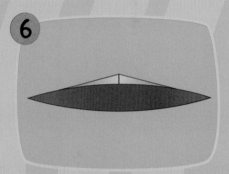

Fold over the outside edges at each side and tape them together.

6

Open your hat and it's ready to wear!

Little Sprout's Vegetable Prints

It's fun to print with vegetables, says Little Sprout! Here are some vegetables you can try printing with.

You will need:
* Poster paints
* Plates
* Cut-up vegetables (see list for ideas)
* Large sheets of paper

1 Ask an adult to cut up an assortment of vegetables and set out plates containing different colors of paint.

2 Make patterns or print a picture using lots of different vegetables, by dipping the vegetables in the paint and pressing them down on the paper.

Vegetables to try:
• Half an apple
• Slices of carrot
• Slices of mushroom
• Half a potato

See #23 for how to cut printing blocks out of potatoes!

Watercress Heads

Grow some green watercress hair in these eggshell heads.

You will need:
* Eggshells
* Felt-tip pens
* Googly eyes
* Potting soil or cotton ball
* Watercress seeds
* Water

1

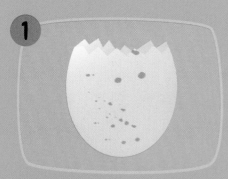

Save the shell after you've eaten a boiled egg, and then carefully clean and dry it.

2

Draw a funny face on the egg with felt-tip pens, or glue on some googly eyes.

3

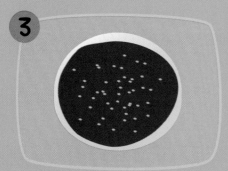

Fill the shell with potting soil or a cotton ball. Add water and sprinkle on some watercress seeds.

4

Put your egghead in a sunny spot and wait for its green watercress hair to grow!

Use your watercress to make some tasty egg-and-watercress sandwiches!

Stand in an egg carton to keep them steady.

107 Plant Some Herbs

Plant a herb garden in a big flowerpot.

You will need:
* Herb seeds
* Flowerpot(s)
* Potting soil
* Craft sticks
* Marker
* Sunshine
* Water

1 Plant the seeds into the potting soil, following the instructions on the packets.

2 Put the flowerpot or pots onto a window ledge.

3 Write the names of the herbs you have planted onto craft sticks and put them in the soil.

4 Remember to water your herbs as they grow!

Some herbs to try:
• mint
• parsley
• chives
• thyme
• oregano
• basil

108 Minty Dip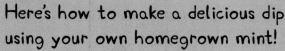

Here's how to make a delicious dip using your own homegrown mint!

You will need:
* Large tub of thick Greek yogurt
* Handful of fresh mint
* 1/4 cucumber
* Knife
* Bowl
* Cheese grater
* Salt and pepper, to taste

1 Ask an adult to slice the cucumber in half lengthwise and remove the seeds with a teaspoon.

2 Ask an adult to grate the cucumber and finely chop the mint into a bowl.

3 Mix in the yogurt with a little salt and pepper.

Serve your minty dip with sticks of crunchy carrots, cucumber, and celery!

If you like the taste, you can add a clove of crushed garlic, too.

Splitter! Splatter!

Make a splatter painting by flicking paint onto a big sheet of paper with a brush.

You will need:
* Paper
* Poster paints
* Paintbrushes
* Water
* Scissors
* Glue

1 Lay out a large sheet of paper.

2 Water down some poster paints, then flick the paint onto the paper with a brush.

Sea background made from splattering lots of different shades of blue paint.

Mummy Pig says this is a good activity to do outside!

Once dry, cut into wavy strips and stick onto some white paper.

Orange splatter-painting fish

Rocket Liftoff

10, 9, 8, 7, 6, 5, 4, 3, 2, 1 . . . Blast off!
Make this rocket and watch it zoom
into space!

You will need:
* Paper
* Scissors
* Colored paints, pens, or pencils
* Drinking straw
* Glue

1 Use the template to draw and cut out two identical rocket shapes from the paper.

2 Glue the sides and the top of the rocket together, but not the bottom.

3 Color your rocket with poster paints, felt-tip pens, or colored pencils.

4 Push the end of a straw into the bottom of the rocket.

Blow through the straw to make your rocket blast off!

template

Space Mobile

Use the templates to make this space mobile to hang in your bedroom.

You will need:
* Cardboard
* Scissors
* Paints
* Paintbrush
* Ribbon or string
* Hole punch
* Wooden chopsticks

1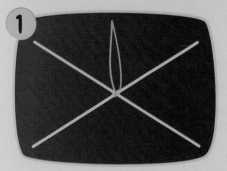

Wrap ribbon or string around the center of two wooden chopsticks to tie them together at right angles.

2

Copy or trace the templates onto cardboard. Cut out the shapes, then paint or color both sides.

3

Use a hole punch to make holes in the tops of the shapes. Attach the shapes to the chopsticks with ribbon or string, then hang the mobile from the ceiling.

moon template

star template

planet template

rocket template

112 Make Up a Space Story

Blast off! One day, two daring astronauts took off into space in their rocket and landed on the moon. They stepped out of their rocket and discovered . . .

Make up a space story about what the brave astronauts found on the moon.

Space Picture

Make this colorful picture of a rocket whizzing through space, past the stars and planets.

You will need:
* Paper
* Crayons
* Black watercolor paint
* Paintbrush

1

Use your crayons to create a space picture on a sheet of paper, using lots of bright colors. Try to fill the whole page.

2

When you've finished,
brush black paint over
the whole paper to see
the colors stand out.

114 Pizza Faces

Peppa and her friends are having a pizza party! Here's how to make some funny pizza faces.

You will need:
* Pizza dough
* Tomato sauce
* Toppings (see box for ideas)

1

Make and roll out pizza dough, or use ready-made pizza dough.

2

Spread a thin layer of tomato sauce onto each base.

3

Add your favorite toppings to make a funny face or a pattern.

4 Ask a grown-up to bake each pizza in a preheated oven at 350°F–400°F for 8–10 minutes.

Pizza toppings

Pineapple chunks
Sliced mozzarella
Peppers
Olives

Sweet corn
Sliced tomatoes
Grated cheddar
Sliced mushrooms

Halloween Lanterns

Make a scary pumpkin lantern to frighten
your friends at Halloween!

1

Ask an adult to cut the top off a
large pumpkin.

2
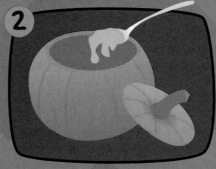
Scoop out the soft insides and
seeds with a spoon.

3

Draw a spooky Halloween
face on the front.

4

Ask an adult to cut out the eyes,
nose, and mouth.

5

Put a night-light inside,
ready for Halloween.

You can carve
a watermelon
if you don't have
a pumpkin.

Ask an
adult to light the
candle when it
gets dark.

Make Up a Halloween Story

Peppa and George have been invited to
a Halloween party with all their friends.
"Let's tell spooky stories," says Peppa.
"You start, Peppa," says Suzy Sheep.
"Once upon a time, a wicked witch turned
a little pig into a frog . . . ," says Peppa.
George looks worried.
What happens next?

117 Spooky Bats

Hang up a chain of spooky black bats at Halloween.

You will need:
* Black paper or poster board
* Tape or glue
* Scissors

1 Glue or tape together 3–4 sheets of black paper or poster board, attaching them along the short edges.

2 Fold the poster board into an accordion, with each fold measuring 6 in.

3 Copy or trace the bat template and draw the bat shape on the top sheet of paper or poster board.

4 Make sure the wings reach the edges of the poster board. Cut out your bats, taking care not to cut the ends of the wings.

5 Open your chain of Halloween bats.

template

Make more bats and glue them together into one really long chain!

See #71 for how to make an accordion.

Witch's Cloak

Dress up as a witch this Halloween.
Here's how to make a black witch's cloak.

You will need:
* Black fabric
* Silver fabric or poster board covered in aluminum foil
* Pinking shears
* Black ribbon or tape
* Fabric glue
* Measuring tape
* Clothespins or large paper clips

Taking measurements

Measure how long you want the cloak to be, from the back of the neck to the hem.

Next, measure from the neck to the wrist.

Double both measurements to cut out the right-sized piece of fabric for the cloak.

1

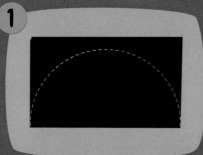

Fold the fabric in half, then cut out a large semicircle, using pinking shears so the fabric does not fray.

2

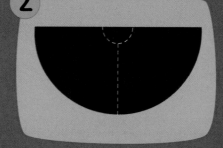

Cut a shallow neckline and a slit down the center of the top layer of fabric.

3

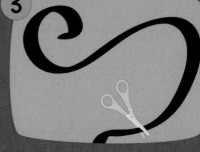

Cut a piece of black ribbon, long enough to go around the neck, plus an extra 15 in.

4

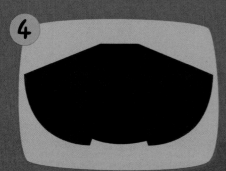

Drizzle fabric glue along the inside edge of the neck, and fold the fabric down over the ribbon and glue, leaving 8 in free at each side.

5

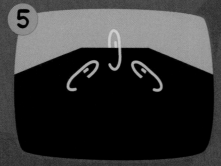

Hold the fabric and ribbon together with large paper clips or clothespins while the glue dries.

6

Cut stars and a moon out of silver fabric and glue them onto the cloak, or glue on poster board shapes covered in aluminum foil.

Witch's Hat

Don't forget to make a witch's hat like Candy Cat's!

You will need:
* Scissors
* Compass
* Glue
* Black construction paper and black poster board
* Aluminum foil
* Ruler
* Pencil

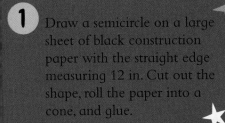

1 Draw a semicircle on a large sheet of black construction paper with the straight edge measuring 12 in. Cut out the shape, roll the paper into a cone, and glue.

2

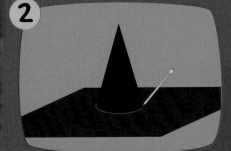

Trace the bottom of the cone onto a piece of black poster board.

3

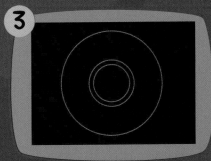

Draw a circle 5 in bigger and another circle 1 in smaller.

4

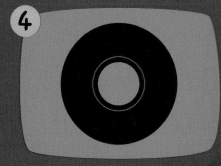

Cut out the large circle, then cut out the small circle, as shown.

5

Cut lines from the inside of the circle to the pencil line, then fold up the tabs.

6

Dab glue onto the tabs and attach the brim to the bottom of the cone.

7

Glue a aluminum foil crescent moon and lots of silver stars onto your witch's hat.

120 Meringue Ghosts

These crunchy ghost meringues are perfect for a Halloween party.

You will need:
* 2 eggs
* Pinch of salt
* 1/2 cup granulated sugar
* Raisins or candied cherries
* Parchment paper

To separate the egg whites:

Crack an egg in half and pour the yolk from one half of the shell to the other, letting the white fall into a bowl.

1 Beat the whites of the eggs and a pinch of salt in a bowl with a whisk until the mixture forms soft peaks.

2 Whisk the sugar into the egg whites a little at a time until the meringue looks glossy white.

3 Lay a sheet of parchment paper over a baking tray. Spread tablespoonfuls of mixture onto the parchment paper.

4 Bake the ghosts for 4–5 hours in an oven at its lowest setting until the meringue mixture is firm. Allow to cool on the tray before enjoying.

Shape the mixture into ghost shapes with the back of a teaspoon.

Give your ghosts tiny raisin eyes and, if you like, sliced cherry mouths.

Putting the oven on its lowest setting keeps the meringues white, like ghosts!

121 Spooky Spider

This black yarn pom-pom spider is perfect for Halloween!

You will need:
* Blue poster board
* Scissors
* Black yarn
* Black elastic
* Googly eyes
* Black pipe cleaners
* Glue

Make a black yarn pom-pom (see #47). Here, instead of tying yarn between the poster board circles, use a long piece of elastic so the spider can bounce up and down.

Cut out a semicircle in blue poster board for a smiley mouth.

Glue on two googly eyes and eight bendy black pipe-cleaner legs.

Hang your pom-pom spider in the corner of a room to make someone jump!

Sock Puppet

This stripy red dragon puppet is made from an old sock!

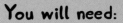

You will need:
* Old sock
* Scissors
* Felt or craft foam
* Fabric glue
* Googly eyes
* Colored felt-tip pens
* Pipe cleaner
* Duct tape

1

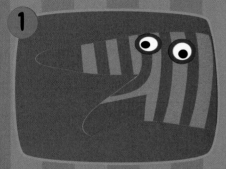

Cut two circles from colored felt or craft foam, slightly larger than your googly eyes. Glue the eyes to these circles and then glue them to the front of the sock, almost opposite the heel.

2

Cut seven small triangles from white felt or craft foam. Glue three to the bottom of the mouth opening and four to the top of the mouth opening to make the teeth.

3

Cut two large triangles from colored felt or craft foam, and glue them along the top edge of the sock, behind the eyes.

4

Cut out two wing shapes from colored felt or craft foam. Using a dark pen, draw on the wing spines to define the shape. Glue one wing on either side of the sock about halfway down the sock length.

5

Twist the end of a pipe cleaner to create the forked tongue, then poke the opposite end through the mouth opening between the toes and the heel.

6 Adjust the pipe cleaner to the desired length and trim the end, making sure no sharp wire sticks out. Then attach inside the sock using either glue or duct tape.

When gluing on all the components, it helps to put the sock on your hand to get everything in the right position.

123 Paper-Plate Fish

These funky fish have been made out of paper plates!

You will need:
* Paper plates
* Scissors
* Glue
* Paint
* Paintbrush
* Tissue paper
* White, black, and colored poster board

Cut a triangle out of the paper plate to make the fish's open mouth.

Glue the triangle onto the back of the plate to make the fish's tail.

Paint your fish bright colors.

To make the fish scales, fold a sheet of tissue paper in half several times. Cut out an oval shape, separate the pieces, and glue onto the body.

Cut out circles of colored, white, and black poster board and stick one on top of the other for the fish's eye.

124 Daddy Pig's Orange Cheesecake

Daddy Pig and George are making a no-bake cheesecake, decorated with tasty little pieces of orange.

1 Put all the graham crackers into a plastic freezer bag and crush them with a rolling pin until they look like fine breadcrumbs. Pour them into a large bowl.

2 Prepare the gelatin using the instructions on the packet, then set to one side. Whisk the cream in a separate bowl until it forms soft peaks.

3 Add the melted butter to the crushed crackers and mix together. Pour the mixture into the pan, press down firmly, then put it in the fridge.

4 Mix the melted chocolate, cream cheese, and orange zest in another bowl until smooth. Add 3 tablespoons of prepared gelatin, mix well, then fold in the whipped cream.

5 Remove the pan from the fridge. Pour the filling on top of the cracker base, then put the pan back in the fridge for an hour, until the topping sets.

6 After an hour, make 1-1/4 cups of orange gelatin using the instructions on the packet. Leave the gelatin to cool, then pour it on top of the cheesecake. Put the cheesecake back in the fridge until the gelatin has set.

You will need:
* 1-1/4 cups gingersnaps, crushed
* 1-1/4 cups graham crackers crushed
* 9-inch springform pan
* 1/2 cup butter (1 stick), melted
* Plastic freezer bag
* Whisk
* Rolling pin
* Mixing bowls

To make the filling:
* 1-1/2 tablespoons powdered gelatin
* 1-2/3 cups heavy cream
* 2 cups white chocolate, melted
* 1-2/3 cups cream cheese
* Zest of one orange
* 1-1/4 cups orange gelatin (made from orange gelatin powder)
* 15-ounce can of orange slices

Carefully take the cheesecake out of the pan and decorate it with orange segments. Yum yum! Snort!

For a vegetarian version, use a vegetarian gelatin substitute instead of powdered gelatin for the filling, and leave off the orange-gelatin topping.

125 Feed the Birds

Make a feeding ball to feed the birds in the wintertime.

You will need:
* Leftover dry kitchen scraps, such as oats, raisins, bread, cake, peanuts, or grated cheese
* Butter (around half the amount of the dry mixture)
* Saucepan
* Wooden spoon
* String

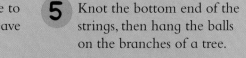

1 Mix your dry ingredients in a bowl.

2 Melt some butter in a saucepan, pour it over the dry mixture, and stir it together.

3 When the mixture has cooled, shape it into balls around long pieces of string.

4 Put the balls in the fridge to set for several hours or leave them overnight.

5 Knot the bottom end of the strings, then hang the balls on the branches of a tree.

Falling Snowflakes

These pretty decorations are easy to make.

You will need:
* Square sheets of white paper
* Scissors
* Pencil
* White thread
* Tape

Every snowflake that falls is unique, which means they all look different!

1. Fold a sheet of paper in half, then in half again to make a smaller square.

2. On the open side, cut a curve from one corner to the other so that, if you opened the paper out, you would have a rough circle.

3. Keeping the paper folded, draw some random shapes on one side, then cut them out.

4. Unfold the paper to reveal your pretty snowflake.

5. Tape a piece of white thread to the top of your snowflake and hang them around the room or on your Christmas tree.

127 Snowy Scene

Make a magic snowy-scene picture!

You will need:
* Paper
* White crayon
* Blue paint
* Paintbrush
* Colored pencils

It's MAGIC!

Use colored pencils to draw the trees and details such as the antenna, windows, and door.

1 Use a white crayon to draw a picture of a snowy day on a sheet of white paper. Make sure you draw lots of big white snowflakes!

2 When you've finished, paint the paper with some watery blue paint and see your picture appear.

128 Build a Snowman

Look! It's snowing! Peppa and George have built a snowman. Next time it snows where you live, why not build a snowman, too?

1 Roll a big ball of snow for the snowman's body.

2 Roll a smaller ball for the snowman's head and put it on top.

3 Use two pebbles or lumps of charcoal for the snowman's eyes, a carrot for his nose, and some twigs for his arms.

4 Wrap a woolly scarf around your snowman's neck and pop a woolly hat on his head!

129 Snowman Faces

Make some fun paper-plate snowman faces to put on your wall.

You will need:
* Scissors
* Paper plate
* White tissue paper or cotton balls
* Glue
* Orange felt or poster board
* Black buttons
* Black and colored poster board or construction paper

Don't forget to give your snowman a hat and scarf!

Hat cut from green poster board or construction paper

Green poster board scarf

1
Glue cotton balls or scrunched-up balls of white tissue paper all over your paper plate.

2
Glue on a piece of orange poster board or felt, cut into a triangle, for the snowman's nose.

3
Add two black button eyes and a mouth of glued-on buttons or poster board circles.

130 Granny Pig's Apple and Blackberry Crumble

This tasty crumble is perfect on a cold winter's day!

For the crumble:
* 2-1/2 cups all-purpose flour
* 1 cup granulated sugar
* 1 cup butter, cubed

For the filling:
* 2 cups chopped apples
* 1 cup blackberries
* 1/4 cup sugar

1 Rub the butter into the flour with your fingertips, so the mixture looks like fine breadcrumbs, then stir in the sugar.

2 Ask an adult to help peel the apples, remove the cores, then cut into 1/2 in pieces. Wash the blackberries, then pat dry.

3 Put the fruit into a greased 9-inch ovenproof dish. Sprinkle the sugar over the fruit, then pour the crumble mixture over the top.

4 Bake the crumble in a preheated oven at 350°F for 40–45 minutes or until the top is golden brown.

Granny Pig says . . .
If you like, add a sprinkle of cinnamon over the fruit mixture before you add the crumble mix.

Serve your apple and blackberry crumble with ice cream, thick cream, or custard. Yum!

131 Penguin Pals

These cute little penguins are
made from toilet-paper rolls.

You will need:
* Toilet-paper rolls
* Black poster paint
  or acrylic paint
* Paintbrush
* Googly eyes
* White paper
* Orange and black
  poster board
* Glue
* Scissors

1 Paint some toilet-paper rolls with black paint.

2 When the paint is dry, glue on a white paper chest and a pair of googly eyes.

penguin wings and feet template

Cut wings from black poster board.

Stick on two orange poster-board feet and an orange beak!

Mini Christmas Tree

Make this mini Christmas tree from a cone of poster board. Don't forget to put the star on top!

You will need:
* Green poster boar[d]
* Large plate
* Pencil
* Ruler
* Scissors
* Glue or tape
* Stick-on gems
* Ribbon
* Aluminum foil

1

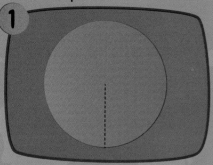

Trace a plate onto green poster board, then cut a line to the center.

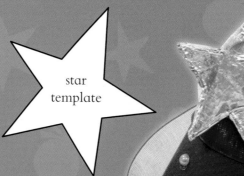

star template

2

Twist the poster board into a cone shape and stick the edges together.

3

Glue some ribbon around the tree, then add some stick-on gems.

4 Copy the star template onto poster board, cover it in foil, then glue it on top.

Peppa sings . . .

"Sweet little star on the Christmas tree goes twinkle, twinkle, twinkle, twee!"

Christmas Tree Decorations

Use cookie cutters to make these decorations to hang on your Christmas tree!

See #24 for instructions on how to make salt dough.

You can also make these decorations using self-hardening modeling clay.

gold glitter tinsel

stick-on gems

swirls of silver glitter

You will need:
* Salt dough
* Rolling pin
* Cookie cutters (star, tree, circle)
* Toothpick
* Poster paints
* Glue
* Water
* Ribbon or yarn
* Glitter
* Stick-on gems

1 Roll out some salt dough with a rolling pin around 1/4 in thick.

2 Cut trees, stars, and circles out of the dough with cookie cutters.

3 Make holes in the top of each decoration with a toothpick.

4 Bake until hard, and leave to cool. Paint, leave to dry, then varnish and decorate.

5 Loop yarn or ribbon through the holes to hang them on your tree.

See #46 for how to varnish.

134 Snowman

Make a little snowman out of clay, small enough to fit in a glittery snow globe!

You will need:
* Oven-hardening modeling clay—green, orange, black, and white
* Water
* Toothpicks

1

Roll out two balls of white clay, making one slightly smaller than the other.

2

Join the balls with a little water. Using the colored clay, give your snowman a hat, scarf, eyes, mouth, and carrot nose.

3

Make two gloves and place them on the ends of toothpicks. Push the toothpicks into the sides of the snowman's body. Bake the snowman in the oven according to the instructions on the packet.

Snow Globe

Pop your clay snowman into a globe made from a plastic jar and shake it to make it snow!

You will need:
* Plastic jar with screw-on lid
* Very strong glue
* Clay snowman or a small toy
* Glitter
* Glycerin
* Water

1 Ask an adult to stick your snowman to the inside of the jar's lid using very strong glue. Thicken some water with glycerin, pour the mixture in the jar, then add some glitter.

2 Screw on the lid and give your globe a shake!

136 Felt Christmas Stocking

Make this little felt Christmas stocking to hang on your Christmas tree!

1 Copy or trace the template onto poster board and cut out two stocking shapes in red felt.

You will need:
* Poster board
* Scissors
* Fabric glue
* Red, white, and green felt
* Gems or silver snowflakes
* Ribbon

2 Cut out a rectangle of white felt to fit the top of the stocking.

Decorate your stocking with silver snowflakes or gems.

3 Glue the felt pieces together with fabric glue. Glue the strip of white felt across the top.

4 Cut some ribbon and glue inside the top of the stocking to make a hanging loop.

Add some green felt in the shape of a triangle to look just like a Christmas tree!

felt Christmas stocking template

Make Up a Christmas Story

It's Christmas Eve, and the house is quiet and still. What's that noise?

Peppa tiptoes downstairs and there, in the living room, is Santa . . . and he's fast asleep!

"Wake up, Santa," cries Peppa. "You still have lots of presents to deliver!"
"Oh dear!" says Santa. "Please will you help me, Peppa?"
Make up a story about Peppa helping Santa deliver presents to her friends.

Action-Hero Cape

Look at Pedro Pony dressed as an action hero. Here's how to make your very own cape, like Pedro's.

You will need:
* Old, adult-sized T-shirt
* Scissors
* Felt or scrap of fabric
* Glue

1 Cut down the side seams and around the armholes of the T-shirt, leaving the neckband intact.

front

back

2 Cut a hero symbol out of felt and glue it onto the back of the T-shirt. Copy Pedro's or Peppa's action-hero symbols or make up your own!

Action-Hero Wristbands

Make some matching wristbands to go with your cape.

You will need:
* Toilet-paper rolls
* Scissors
* Paints
* Paintbrush
* Silver poster board
* Glue

1 Cut the toilet-paper rolls to make two lengths, about 2 in long. Cut down the sides of the rolls so they open out slightly.

2 Paint the rolls to match your cape. When the paint is dry, paint or glue on a matching action-hero symbol and some shiny silver bands made from poster board.

140 Action-Hero Mask

Now make an action-hero mask!

You will need:
* Black poster board
* Scissors
* Darning needle
* Black elastic

1 Copy or trace the template below onto black poster board and cut it out.

template

2 Cut out the eyeholes and make small holes in the sides of the mask with a darning needle.

3 Thread black elastic through the holes, measure to fit, then knot the elastic at each side.

Make Up an Action-Hero Story

It is a quiet day at Madame Gazelle's playgroup and everyone is busy painting.

"Help! Help!" someone shouts from outside the window.
Oh no, it's Dr. Hamster. Her pet, Tiddles the tortoise, is stuck up a tree!

Don't panic! It's Pedro the action hero to the rescue! Make up a story about how Pedro saves the day!

Princess Peppa Book Cover

Cover one of your favorite books or notebooks, so it looks just like Peppa's princess book!

You will need:
* Sheets of dark pink and gold wrapping paper
* Scissors
* Glue
* Colored pom-poms or stick-on gems

1

Open the book, lay it on the inside of a sheet of pink wrapping paper, then cut the paper so it is 1-1/2 to 2 in bigger than the book.

2

Cut diagonal lines from the edge of the paper to the center of the book. Throw away the triangles of paper in the middle.

3

Fold over one side of the paper to fit the front cover of the book, then do the same at the back.

4

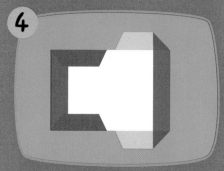

Fold down a triangle of paper in each corner, then fold over the edges and glue in place.

Use this template to cut out a gold Peppa crown to glue onto the book's new cover!

template

Decorate the crown with stick-on gems or colored pom-poms.

Now you have a princess book that looks just like Peppa's!

All About Me Book

Start a scrapbook all about YOU!

Buy a blank notebook, or make one from folded sheets of colored construction paper. Glue in photos of yourself, your family, and your friends, tickets to places you've visited, wrappers of your favorite sweets, pictures of your favorite animals, and some of your drawings.

You will need:
* Construction paper
* Pencil
* Darning needle
* Yarn or thick string

To make a scrapbook:

1 Fold 5–6 sheets of construction paper in half.

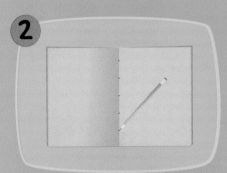

2 Make a mark in the center of the spine. Then make two marks above and below this mark.

3 Push a needle through all the marks to make holes.

4

Thread a darning needle with yarn or thick string. Push the needle through the center hole, from the inside out, then sew in and out of the holes, following the letters on the drawing, ending with the yarn coming out of the middle hole. Tie the ends of the yarn together in a knot.

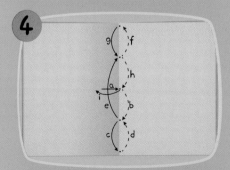

144 Sunflower Height Chart

Measure how tall you are growing on a giant sunflower height chart!

You will need:
* Long sheet of paper, such as kraft paper
* Paints
* Paintbrush
* Green poster board or paper
* Scissors
* Reusable adhesive putty

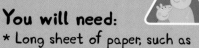

1 Paint a big sunflower with a long green stem on a sheet of kraft paper and fix it to the wall.

2 Cut out some big green sunflower leaves.

3 Measure everyone's height against the sunflower stem and make a mark on the paper.

4 Write each person's name on a leaf and stick it onto the sunflower stem to show how tall they are.

5 Measure everyone's height again in a few months' time to see how much they have grown!

145 Handprint Trees

Use your hands to print some colorful trees!

You will need:
* Paper
* Paint
* Big paintbrush
* Your hands!

Paint your hand with brown paint and press it onto a sheet of paper to make the tree's trunk and branches.

Dab on blobs of paint with a big brush or your fingertips to give your tree pink blossoms, green leaves, or orange and gold autumn colors.

146 Handprint Animals

You can also use your hands to make animal pictures.

Make the head and neck the same color as your handprint. Then paint some orange legs and a beak.

Use different colors of paint to give your fish stripes.

Give your animals eyes and a smiley mouth with a black felt-tip pen.

147 Kazoo Comb

It's fun to make your own musical instruments, like this kazoo comb.

Fold a sheet of tissue paper over a large wide-toothed comb. Press your lips against the tissue-paper comb and hum!

148 Water Music

Fill glasses or jam jars with different amounts of water. Tap the glasses with a pencil or a metal spoon and listen to the different sounds!

If you like, add a few drops of food coloring to each glass to make the water different colors.

149 Maracas

These marvelous maracas are made from plastic bottles!

1 Make sure your plastic bottles are clean and dry, then pour in something that will make a noise when you shake it.

2 Screw on the bottle caps, put a toilet-paper roll over the top of each bottle, and tape in place.

3 Cut lengths of masking tape or duct tape, and wind around the roll to make a handle.

You will need:
* Clear plastic bottles
* Toilet-paper rolls
* Scissors
* Colored masking tape or duct tape
* Paper clips, beads, dried peas, or lentils
* Colored ribbons

Fill each bottle about half full.

Get busy shaking!

Tie colored ribbons around the top of the handle to decorate.

Chocolate Puddle Biscuits

Shape these tasty boot biscuits out of cookie dough and dip them in chocolate puddles! Yum! Yum!

1 Preheat the oven to 350°F and lightly grease a flat baking tray.

2 Mix together the butter and sugar, mix in the egg yolks, then stir in the flour.

3 Add just enough milk to bring the mixture together into a soft dough.

4 Sprinkle some flour onto a work surface. Divide the ball of dough into three pieces, divide each ball in half, then in half again, to make 12 balls.

5 Roll out each ball into a sausage shape. Turn up the bottom of each sausage and press it flat to make a boot shape.

6 Bake the biscuit boots for 10–15 minutes, until golden brown. Sprinkle with sugar, then leave to cool.

You will need:
* 1/2 cup butter (1 stick), softened
* 1/2 cup granulated sugar, plus extra for sprinkling
* 2 egg yolks
* 1-2/3 cups all-purpose flour, sifted
* 1-2 tablespoons milk
* Large bar of milk chocolate

Makes 12 biscuit boots

Dip the boots in the cooled muddy chocolate puddle—and eat! Snort!

Melt a large bar of milk chocolate in a microwave or over a pan of simmering water, then pour the chocolate into a shallow bowl.

Peppa loves muddy puddles, especially when they're made of chocolate!